NAUGHTY NORA

Star Lovers - Book Two

LYS BRITDOTTER

Published by Blushing Books
An Imprint of
ABCD Graphics and Design, Inc.
A Virginia Corporation
977 Seminole Trail #233
Charlottesville, VA 22901

Lys Britdotter
Naughty Nora

eBook ISBN: 978-1-64563-916-9
Print ISBN: 978-1-64563-917-6
v2

Chapter 1

The 2010 Malibu sped down Route 29 with reckless abandon. The road was bumpy and dark, an asphalt ribbon that tied together one little farm community with another. The night was clear, with the half moon rising, so the occupants of the Malibu were making good time. At the wheel was Jessie Laurance, the owner, who was speeding as if there was no tomorrow, and next to her, in the front passenger seat, slumped Nora Dawson. Nora was gravely injured, and the thought crossed her mind that perhaps there was no tomorrow, at least for her.

Nora Dawson Glower was used to fear and suffering, but tonight was a whole new ball game.

Nora was very near to total collapse, her injured body held up by her seat belt. Each bump coursed through Nora's broken body with excruciating pain. She gritted her teeth and tried not to moan, but each swerve, each pothole, sent shudders of agony through her body

Every gasping attempt to take a deep breath felt as if someone was stabbing her with a butcher knife. Now, halfway to the hospital, she gave up and resorted to little gasps, but even those feeble attempts to take in oxygen made her eyes fill with tears. Still, considering the injuries she had just suffered at the hands of her brute of an ex-husband, she was barely making a sound.

Her best friend, Jessie, sensed her desperation and took one hand off the wheel and patted Nora's hand. Jessie was driving like a maniac, pushing her old Malibu to the limit to reach the hospital in Eastwood.

"Don't worry. I'll have you at the hospital in no time."

To make matters worse, Nora's mental pain was even greater than the physical; she was overcome with guilt that her problems had placed her good friends in harm's way. Jessie, in the driver's seat, was trying to save her life, and Gilly and Rose, in the back seat, were calling out encouragement.

It had always been this quartet since kindergarten, the four of them, Jessie, Nora, Gilly and Rose, watching out after each other. Now, all these years later, they were being pursued by Nora's maniac ex-husband, Dale Glower, and his equally crazy best friend, Jimmy Brady.

To make Nora's guilt even greater, in her lap rested her injured dog. Muffin was half conscious, another incidental victim of Dale Glower's uncontrolled rage. Every few minutes the poor little mutt spasmed with little shudders and Nora petted his ear with one finger. The rest of her hand was smashed where Dale had used her as a stomping board.

Her ex-husband had vowed to kill her, and tonight, he almost succeeded. In fact, perhaps it was too soon to tell. She was pretty sure several ribs were broken from his kicks, and she was seeing double, which was a sign of a concussion. When she inhaled, she could taste blood; her lower lip was definitely split.

"Hang in there, Nora!" Gilly kept saying over and over.

Of the four of them, Gilly was the fighter. Jessie was the "thinker" and Rose, quiet Rose, was the gentle healer, soothing over angry feelings and scraped knees when they were kids. No wonder she became a nurse.

And Nora? She had always been the "mother figure," the nurturer. Just like her Swedish-born mom, Berga Stiven Dawson, quiet, loving, forgiving. But those had brought her mother to an early death. Was it going to be the same for her?

"I'm looking over my shoulder and I see headlights, Jessie," Gilly called out. "Put the pedal to the metal!"

"I already am," Jessie said with gritted teeth. "I'm driving at the Malibu's limit."

"Why do car chases seem so exciting in a movie, but are so scary in real life?" Rose wondered out loud.

Of all of them, Rose sounded the calmest, which was a surprise since she was so timid. Perhaps they had miscalculated. After all, Rose was an emergency room nurse. She dealt with trauma every day. It was Rose who ordered Jessie to drive to the neighboring town because the hospital in Eastwood was better than the one in Ridge Valley, their own little farm town smack in the middle of the state of Ohio.

"Everything seems better in a movie." Gilly laughed. "Don't worry, Rose. We'll keep you safe."

"I don't need to be kept safe, Gilly! I'm a grown woman. How is Muffin doing?"

Nora heard the exasperation in Rose's voice but wasn't able to answer. She saw Jessie take her eyes off the road again and shoot a glance at the pile of fur in Nora's lap and shook her head.

"How is the Muffin doing?" Gilly echoed Rose.

Nora sucked in her breath. She loved Muffin, her rescue stray, and look at the poor thing now!

"That bastard kicked him across the room," she whispered. "I think he's got internal injuries."

"Don't try to talk, Nora," Rose ordered from the back seat.

"Save your breath. You have to keep your oxygen level up. How long until we get her to the hospital, Jessie?"

"About fifteen minutes on the farm road. If I take the short cut, it could easily be ten."

Nora heard the worry in their voices and felt a tear slip out of her battered eye. How could she have been so stupid, so careless as to let Dale get to her? Their divorce had been finalized six months ago!

And it had been a tough day for other reasons. Her father, who had abandoned her and her mother years ago, had left a note on her front door. He wanted a loan, of course. The minute she had seen his handwriting, the food in her stomach had done a flip-flop and she had spent the next fifteen minutes in the bathroom, heaving up all the bad memories she had suppressed of Angus Dawson.

It had taken her a while to get a grip. She wasn't a little girl anymore; she was a woman! Tonight, with her closest friends, she would figure out how to handle the unwelcomed reappearance. Finally, full of pep talk, she had finally started to relax. That was the big mistake. Never lower your guard. Didn't her whole life teach her that?

She had been happily singing a popular tune she had memorized, when Dale smashed through the front door and caught her at home, getting ready to go out for pizza with her best buds, and being Dale, he immediately thought she had a hot date. Her words of protest, "I'm only meeting the girls," fell on deaf ears. He wanted a fight, and he was a big man, six three and almost three hundred pounds. The last hundred he had gained in the three years of their marriage.

"All dolled up, Nora." He had circled her unsteadily, his bleary red eyes taking in every detail, his voice accusing. He flexed his fists like a boxer preparing a punch, and Nora saw the new tattoo on his bulging left bicep. It was a skeletal face with blood dripping from the mouth. "What's the matter? You don't like my new art?"

Nora shrugged. What this moron did with his rapidly decaying body wasn't her problem anymore. But Dale kept circling and she was getting scared.

"Silver-blonde hair, straight as silk, a little chubby, but in all the right places. That black mini skirt and red blouse look pretty sexy. Whoa! Black high heels and no stockings!" He lumbered around, closing the distance between them.

"It's August and eighty-five degrees outside," Nora snapped with unexpected irritation.

He ignored her valid argument. "Hoping you're going to pick up some bad boy and bring him home?"

"Get out of here, Dale! We are divorced. You don't live here anymore." She had pointed to the door with a bravado she didn't feel.

His reaction was instantaneous. He crossed the distance to her with his hand right raised and smacked her across the face. Muffin began to bark and nip at his boots. The little stray rescue dog was one-part poodle, one-part spaniel, rest unknown. Dale bellowed at the dog, swearing to kill him.

Nora had fought for control and tried to keep calm. Frantically, she tried to think of all the tips the social worker had given her to deal with Dale. *Well, guess what, Miss Social Worker, the tips aren't working*, she'd thought with a nervous laugh.

One more try! Miss Social Worker said to be assertive. "Get out now, or I will call the police."

Dale's response was a punch to the stomach that made her sick. At five foot five, she was no match for Dale.

She desperately gasped for air.

His fist connected with her chin so quickly, she was stunned and fell back onto the couch.

"Get me a beer!" he shouted, looming over her and prodding

her with his boot. Then he had struck out and kicked Muffin. The little dog flew through the air and landed in a heap in the living room before skidding across the kitchen floor and under the table.

Nora had slipped off the couch and crawled to the kitchen on her knees and searched for her cell. She was relieved to find her phone in her skirt pocket. She would use the time to text her waiting friends. She wanted her last words to be with the women who truly loved her. She had just enough time to send out a text.

If she hadn't, she would be a dead woman right now.

Dale had followed her into the kitchen, cursing and swearing, saw the phone, and tried to drag Nora out from under the table. That was when he had stomped on her hand. Her fingers had broken in a sickening crunch, but her resistance had given her friends who were waiting at the pizza parlor right around the corner from Nora's bungalow, just enough time to reach her. They had rushed in with fire in their eyes. Jessie hit Dale in the face with a shovel Nora had left on the front porch, then threw pepper into his eyes. Once he was on the floor, Gilly gave him a well-placed kick to the crotch that sent him rolling and screaming. Meanwhile, Rose, who was a nurse, had found a towel and gone to work on her.

"She needs to go to a hospital pronto!" Nora heard Rose say through a cloud of pain.

"Muffin?" Nora had to struggle to ask.

Gilly and Rose had half-carried, half-dragged her outside and into the waiting car. Jessie followed with Muffin in her arms. They pushed Nora into the passenger seat next to Jessie, who jumped behind the wheel, and Gilly and Rose scrambled into the back seat. Jessie began to back out.

"Shit. I don't believe it!" Jessie sounded so shocked that Nora had forced her swollen eyes open.

To her horror, Dale was outside and staggering toward the rust bucket he called a pickup truck.

Equally dumbfounded, Gilly muttered a curse, "He's coming after us!"

Rose shook her head. "He can't drive in that condition."

"Want to bet!" Jessie cried out, but she was defiant. "I can out race him."

Even as she spoke, Dale was clutching his balls and shaking his fist at them. Nora shuddered. He was truly in a terrible rage. If there was one thing she had learned in her years of marriage, it was that Dale, when in a rage, was a stupid beast.

"Go, girl!" Gilly cried out.

"I'm on my way!" Jessie had called out.

"To Eastwood," Rose said emphatically.

"Eastwood?" Jessie was clearly shocked. "Eastwood is ten miles away?"

"Nine to be exact, but they have an MRI. Our town hospital, Ridge Valley, doesn't. And Nora needs an MRI!" Usually, Rose was so meek, but now she sounded like a no-nonsense nurse.

Jessie hadn't argued. "Eastwood it is."

Unfortunately, the road to Eastwood went past Sinful Sam's, the bar where Dale and Jessie's ex-boyfriend worked as bouncers. Even through her own pain, Nora could hear Jessie groan. Jimmy Brady, Jessie's ex-boyfriend, was outside, talking on his phone.

"There stands Jimmy Brady. All set to join his pal Dale." Jessie confirmed this with a scornful snap.

Jimmy saw and recognized Jessie's car and shook his fist at them.

"Of all the men we could have chosen, Nora, we had to choose those two bastards."

Jimmy was another Dale, but smarter.

Nora couldn't answer. She was getting sick to her stomach and her head was pounding. She felt Rose reach over and place a cool hand on her throat. Her friend was taking her pulse.

This wasn't lost on Jessie. "How is she doing?"

"Just drive!" Rose said quietly.

Jessie continued analyzing the situation. "Best bet, Jimmy's waiting for Dale to pick him up."

"But we have a head start." This was from Gilly in the back seat.

Always defiant, always ready for a fight, Gilly carried a lot of anger in her slim, athletic body.

"Do you really think they'll come after us?" Rose asked.

"Hyenas hunt in packs," Jessie snorted. "Still, we should sing 'when I wish upon a star' for luck to get us to a safe spot."

Jessie began to sing, joined by Rose and Gilly. Gilly started the tradition one night in seventh grade when they ran down the ravine behind her house to escape from a bunch of older boys who were following them too closely.

Nora tried to speak but coughed up some blood instead. This ride was bringing back nightmares from her childhood. How many times had she and her mother driven frantically to get away from her father? Too many. She had sworn her life would be different, and yet here she was, fleeing for her life from a violent man.

How did that happen? How could she not have seen the signs? But asking these questions was pointless now. What was important was the safety of her three best friends. She couldn't let her friends pay for her mistakes. She tried to push herself up in her seat, but her ribs were killing her. She groaned.

"Don't try to speak," Rose admonished gently, patting her shoulder from the back seat.

"I have to!" Nora whispered hoarsely. "This is my fault. I want you to let me out and save yourselves. Please! You don't know what he is capable of doing."

Actually, they had a pretty good idea, but there was no way they were going to do what she asked.

"No way that's going to happen, our naughty little Nora," Gilly teased, trying to distract her. "Naughty Nora ate the cookies!"

Nora tried to smile, but it hurt too much. Even through the pain, she could see her mother smiling when she caught Nora at the cookie jar. That was how the name 'Naughty Nora' came about.

So long ago. Boy, did she miss her mom! If her mother were watching from Heaven, she would be crying her heart out.

"Is there a full moon tonight?" Rose asked her friends.

Jessie said no. The full moon was actually two weeks ago.

"It's awfully bright out, isn't it?" Gilly confirmed Rose's question.

Before Jessie could reply, she swerved to avoid a pothole and it shook Nora out of her memories.

"Who was that?" Rose asked from the back seat. "I think I saw him earlier in the emergency room."

"*What* was it? That's a better question," asked Gilly. "I never saw anyone dressed like that here in Ohio! But there was something familiar about him. I think I might have seen him at the gym."

"He was all in white and his hair matched the color of his clothes!" Jessie couldn't keep the surprise out of her voice. "Anyway, I was going to take the main road, but I think I'll take the road through Creepy Woods instead."

Nora was in too much pain to care. And under her fingers, Muffin's breathing was becoming more ragged and his heart slower. Her poor little dog! Suddenly, she heard a shot ring out and then another.

"Jimmy's shooting at us!" Gilly cried out in warning. "Pedal to the metal, Jessie girl. He's gaining on us."

Rose cursed.

If Rose cursed, then it must be bad, Nora thought with a flicker of humor.

Jessie swore, "Damn! I didn't count on how dark these woods are!"

The rear window exploded. A bullet came through the back and right through her front windshield. When another shot hit the left rear tire of the Malibu, Jessie lost control. Nora felt the car lurch forward. It flew into a ditch and struck a small tree. Nora's injuries made her scream in pain. She could feel the wheels spinning beneath them, and it was clear they were stuck.

It only took a moment for Dale and Jimmy to slam in behind them. The headlights from the truck gave everything a lurid color. Nora could see the dashboard, and the little pile of fur in her lap groaned. The dog seemed to sense the danger.

"Lock the doors," Jessie cried out. But that did little good.

Armed with crowbars, flashlights and a gun, Dale beat on the metal doors. The man was like a grizzly bear having cornered his prey. Dale was powerful and nothing stopped him. He punched out Nora's window with the crowbar, poked his head in, and his hands went around her neck. He grabbed Nora's hair and began to shake her head back and forth. "Think you could get away from me? Never!"

Nora tried to think, but she was too injured and there was so much screaming and confusion. She was aware that Gilly and Rose were pleading for Dale and Jimmy to stop, and Jessie seemed to have fallen out of the driver's side door. Everything was lit up by a strange, luminescent light. Jessie was on her knees in front of Jimmy Brady. As for her, Dale was pulling at her with all his might.

"I'm dragging you right out this window, you bitch," he snarled.

Nora held tight to Muffin, just sensing that the dog didn't

want to leave her side. She fought to stay in the car, but Dale was almost killing her. He had dropped her hair and now reached for her neck. She would be dead soon, she thought. Her neck would snap.

A thought broke through her pain. Maybe if she died, she would see her mother again? And maybe she was already dead.

That strange light was getting brighter.

And suddenly, Dale's grip disappeared, along with his snarling face. She thought she heard him scream. A weird face was peering at her through the broken glass. Something or someone was at the end of the tunnel. Isn't a tunnel what people described in near death experiences? They saw a light at the end of the tunnel. An angel came to greet them.

But do angels have three eyes and... this one did, two sharply blue eyes and one red one in the middle of a large face. The strangling force around her neck had disappeared and she could inhale. The door flew open and she was enveloped in the light.

Muffin came alive for a moment and yelped. Then he sagged in her arms again. Why was she spinning? No. Not spinning. Rushing upward. Gravity didn't seem to work when you were dead, she decided.

Her eyes were now too bruised to open. She could only sag, like Muffin, into the safety of the light. It seemed to support her and lift her at the same time.

She heard a voice, male, melodious, telling her she was going to be fine, whispering endearments of encouragement. It asked her name.

"Naughty Nora," she whispered then realized that wasn't right. She tried to correct it, but the low voice laughed.

"No. That is perfect. I love it. Naughty Nora. Exactly what I needed to find. "

Nora gasped as a warm hand moved between her legs to reposition her body.

"Very nice. I like the way you respond to my touch."

Nora was too far gone with injuries to say anything else. Whoever was holding her chuckled softly and pulled her close. "Naughty Nora," the voice hummed.

A warm hand slid down her belly and slipped proprietarily between her legs.

Even half unconscious, Nora could not suppress a sigh of pleasure at the touch.

"Welcome to my world."

Chapter 2

"Welcome to my world."

Whoever spoke to her wasn't kidding. There was a firmness in his speech that left no doubt about whose world it was.

Later, when she tried to recall the events of that wild night, those words would race through her memory like a pleasant shock. The words were as clear as a bell.

When she struggled to remember what had happened in the hours that followed her rescue from Dale, everything but those words were a haze. There was a vague memory of powerful arms lifting her from the ground, a bright light that pulled her away from Earth and ended at the entrance of some kind of hovering spacecraft.

Perhaps it was because she had experienced the worst that humanity had to offer that she wasn't frightened. Or perhaps it was because she was so close to death that anything that was alive was good. Life was whatever it was. The life force was a good thing. Too bad she was dying.

Once she was inside the craft, she was lifted up and placed on an examining table. The lights were bright, and the room was pleasantly warm. Whoever these creatures were, they had taken good care of her, she knew that for sure, and they were as gentle as possible. More than one entity moved around the room. Maybe three? She couldn't tell. The shapes were odd, not human, and she could only see them through the cool astringent cloth placed over her face.

"The medicines in the cloth will ease your pain," a low voice murmured.

Slowly, the agony subsided as gentle hands moved over her body, probing, examining, and evaluating the extent of her injuries. Her rescuers communicated in a language she couldn't understand. It was staccato, like calling out numbers. Every time someone checked a part of her body, there were rapid sounds like beeps, followed by what she guessed were words.

Gasping for breath, she opened her mouth. "My dog… is… he…"

"We are working on him right now. Don't worry."

Nora recognized the voice. It went with the enormous power that had pulled her away from Dale. It was hard to think about it for long. Each time she tried, she just slipped off into a sweet sleep. Whoever had saved her from Dale's beefy fists could have told her she was on Mars and she wouldn't have cared.

"You are safe with me. I promise you." It was the melodious voice, almost a low hum. She felt a firm but warm grip on her hand.

"Tria. Continue."

Who was Tria? Nora wondered vaguely. "Tria?" It came out as a groan of pain.

At the command, another voice, crisp and efficient, broke in. "Don't try to talk, human. We are assessing your injuries. You are leaking from several locations and your life fluid is escaping."

Leaking? In spite of her injuries, Nora's eyes flew open.

The grip on her hand tightened, to comfort her.

"What Tria means is that you are bleeding in your lungs, and you have a serious brain injury. We are going to put you into an induced coma to assist healing. When you awake, we will explain."

There was no arguing with that voice.

Before Nora could force her injured mouth to form words of protest, she felt a slight pressure on her forehead right between her eyes. Without any effort, she began the long spiral into a sweet sleep that would lead to recovery.

Time seemed to lack significance.

Nora hovered on the edge of consciousness. Awareness came slowly, a peaceful unraveling of the dream state into alertness. She was on an examination table, covered with a blanket that molded to her body. The room seemed completely empty. It was like being inside a large can with only an overhead light and her table to fill the space.

Nora realized the towel that had covered her face was gone, and if she opened her eyes, she could look around. First, the ceiling. It was very shiny and there were lights in the metal. She forced herself to go slowly, first turning her neck to the right, then to the left. Back and forth.

Inhaling with caution, she sniffed strange scents which filled her nostrils—something like cinnamon if cinnamon was grown inside a lemon. And she could hear steady ticking sounds. The beats soothed her tremendously.

What was real and what was something she imagined? Was she in a hospital on Earth or in a spacecraft like she remembered? There were no answers she could find to explain what had happened to her.

Carefully, Nora opened her mouth and realized she could easily breath through her nose. Her lungs, surrounded by her rib cage, could take a deep breath without any pain. She lifted her arm and looked at her hand. The one that had been crushed under the heel of Dale's boot seemed absolutely fine. She flexed her fingers and was amazed to see someone had given her a manicure. Pale pink polish had been applied to all her fingers and two thumbs. When she realized that somehow, miraculously, she was fine, she dropped her arm and sighed with relief.

"Satisfied that we fixed you up properly?" The low, teasing voice came out of nowhere.

Nora tried to jerk upright, but powerful hands held her in place.

"Relax. Relax." Someone was standing behind her, holding her shoulders down.

"I thought I was alone," she gasped.

"I was wondering when you would look around and see me."

"I can't see you now," Nora protested. "Just your very large hands."

"Are you ready?" he teased.

"For what?" Nora tried sounding brave and aggressive. It was an act. It was hard when you were restrained with invisible ties, lying on a table in something resembling a soup can.

In response, the alien walked around the table, and she sucked in her breath with shock.

Then her jaw dropped open. Whoever… whatever *it* was, looked almost human except much taller, perhaps nine feet tall, very muscular, and totally hairless. Even though he wore a white lab coat, Nora knew instinctively this was a male. This creature facing her was intensely masculine. No way was she ready for this.

"I told you so." There was strength in his voice but humor, too.

She met his gaze, confused.

"I told you you weren't ready to see me completely, but you were pretty cocky, so I decided to go for it."

Three eyes met her gaze, two very bright blue ones and a red one in the middle. The red one over his small nose reminded her of a calculator. She tried to focus, wondering if she were still unconscious and this was all a dream.

As soon as she managed the question in her mind, the creature shook his head and laughed. "You are very much awake, and I am as real as you are."

"You can read my mind?" Fear flared up in her. How powerful was this creature?

"Yes, right now I can read your mind, but later on I will disconnect that capability. The red diode on your scalp is transmitting all information into our computers."

He guided her hand to her scalp, and she felt something embedded at the hairline. It was about the size of a penny.

"What is this?" Nora demanded fearfully. "Is it a scar from the accident?"

"A chip. Some people call it a sensor. It monitors your brain waves both awake and asleep. It is there to help you heal and to help us with our experiments. It is red, just like mine, but it isn't an eye."

"That's an invasion of privacy," Nora sputtered. "Turn it off right now!"

He didn't answer her at first. He just stared at her as if summing her up. Then he nodded. "I would think that my reading your mind is the least of your problems, but since it upsets you, I will turn off my receptor when it is appropriate. But I must tell you that you are still transmitting data to our computers."

"Don't I have a say in this?"

"No." He laughed, actually surprised at her audacity.

"I remember you from last night," Nora said lamely.

"Actually, it was over two days ago. But I'm glad you remember."

Nora took a deep breath and went for honesty. "Actually, I thought, perhaps, that I had hallucinated."

"I'm very real, as you can see." He put his hands in his lab coat and grew serious. "You were very badly injured. It took us two days to fix you up. Lucky for you, Tria, my assistant, is trained in human repair."

A sudden thought occurred to her and she forgot her fear for herself. "Where is Muffin?" Her gray eyes flashed with concern.

"I was correct. You put your little dog first, before asking about your own safety. Very altruistic of you."

"Muffin?" she repeated.

"We have beamed him to the mother ship, where they are better prepared to care for his injuries. He was very close to death. In fact, he was dead, but we were able to revive him and send him on his way."

"Will he live?" Nora felt an enormous lump in her throat rising to choke her.

"Yes. I think so. Is that important to you?" His blue eyes bored into her face.

"Very." Nora sucked back a sob. "He is all I have in this world. And, of course, my three friends. Did they survive the crash?"

"Oh, yes. Your friend, Jessie, is in a nearby craft. Rose and Gilly are in two other crafts circling Earth, although Gilly might be moved to our undersea operations for a day or two, and Rose will be going to the mother ship for the rest of her stay."

Undersea operations? Mother ship? Spacecraft? This was all too much for her. She struggled to get up and off the table, but some kind of force kept her in place. She couldn't move more than several inches.

"Don't distress yourself. Tria said you were to only rest today."

"Who is Tria, and who are you, and what's going on?" Nora's voice broke with a tremor of sudden anxiety, especially when the creature in front of her took a stool and sat down. He took her hand in his giant one and began to massage her palm. "And you have three eyes and all you are wearing is a long lab coat."

"Good. You can count and you are observant."

"That's pretty insulting!"

"Not meant to be. With humans, we find every possible subgroup. The intelligent, the stupid, the good, the bad, the hysterical, the brave. I can go on forever." He laughed. "By the way, I like the way you show spirit. I think I have a lot to work with when I study you, Naughty Nora."

Naughty Nora? How did he know her nickname?

"You told me," he said matter-of-factly. "You just don't remember. Your exact words were that your name was Nora Dawson Gower, but your friends call you Naughty Nora. That instantly got my attention.

She forgot about the three eyes and focused on the alien's words. "Of all the things that could get your attention, why Naughty Nora?"

"It makes you an interesting study in our research."

"What kind of research? What are you talking about?" Her eyes narrowed. "I thought you saved me?"

"Out of the goodness of my hearts?"

Nora heard the plural and raised her head two inches. "Hearts? How many do you have?"

"Three. Two for every day, and one for a spare. It won't beat unless activated. And, to answer your question, yes, I'm glad I was there to rescue you from that brute, but I have agendas of my own. I was out looking for young women."

Nora slammed her head back down on the pillow and closed her eyes. Just her damn luck! She was never lucky with men! This creature that had saved her from Dale was going to kill her. "You're a serial killer!"

The red eye blinked rapidly and the creature burst out laughing with such force, Nora felt the table wobble. There was a lot of strength and power in this alien, she realized. His blue eyes were sending out sparks of good humor, but he was powerful enough to twist Dale Gower into a pretzel. Perhaps he had. She was suddenly afraid to ask.

"Really, Nora? A serial killer?" One of his hands reached out and stroked her silky hair. It was a gentle gesture but virile and intimate at the same time. "In all the studies I have performed, you are the first woman to accuse me of that horrible crime."

His voice was lyrical, as if his vocal cords were a musical instrument. Nora had the feeling he was enjoying her discomfort. He was regarding her intently.

"Do you think we Eluvians traveled across space and time just to kill you?"

"How should I know what to think?" Nora gulped. "I'm trying to figure this all out. And you are so tall. I have to crane my neck to see your face."

"Well, I can't help that. You will just have to get used to it. But let me help you out with the rest."

The alien leaned in closer. His skin was a peachy color and gave off the scent of something wild, like a summer morning in the tropics. "First of all, you were being chased by your ex-husband, who had brutally beaten both you and your little dog. Do you remember that?"

How could she forget? Tears welled up in her eyes, but something else, too. There was anger. Anger at Dale, anger at her father, and anger that she was sitting here naked and helpless.

He also picked up on the anger. "Why are you angry?" He tugged at the strand of silky hair and let it slip through his fingers, but the three eyes never left her face.

She ignored the question. She looked closely at the alien. "Are you sure you aren't going to kill me?"

"Of course not. In fact, we have gone to a lot of trouble to keep you alive. Jessie wasn't too badly injured, and Rose and Gilly were fine, but you needed lung repair, jawbone reconstruction, and replacement of all the bones in your left hand. Not to mention a new rib insertion."

Nora lifted her left hand and stared at it. It looked perfect. She flexed it in awe.

"How long did this take?" she asked in a whisper.

"In Earth time, it took forty-eight hours, to be exact, but Tria has ordered that we not commence the experiments until tomorrow. The reconstructive glues and adhesives must set."

To her complete mortification, he lifted the blanket and peaked at her naked body. Nora watched as his blue eyes studied her breasts and then slowly moved to her belly and then to the little triangle of hair between her legs. Then he dropped the blanket and smiled.

"Very nice," he whispered. "You are healing nicely."

Tria's instructions, or not, Nora recognized desire in his blue eyes as he studied her. Panic overcame her and she tried to sit up.

"Don't do that!" The lilting voice was gone, replaced with one of steel. The alien commanded with such force that she stopped struggling and fell back. "It won't work. You're tied down for your own protection."

To her surprise, he reached out and began to slowly massage her shoulders while still talking. "I am in charge, Nora, and you will listen carefully to what I say." When she didn't speak, he gave her face the lightest of slaps. "Are you listening? This is very important."

"You were telling me about the experiments and studies. What did you mean?" Even as she asked, she was suddenly, painfully, aware that she was stark naked and his touch, gentle, yet strong, was sensual and carnal. She couldn't help taking a deep breath.

She noticed the red light on his face blinking rapidly again. Was he picking up on her pleasure? She wanted to ask, but pride kept her silent. She felt a little buzz on her scalp and her hand flew to her head. "Will you please tell me what is going on? Who are you?"

"I believe you humans refer to us as aliens and our crafts as UFOs."

"Unbelievable."

"Not at all. When and if you humans get off planet Earth and land someplace else in the universe, you will be the aliens. I am an IHB."

Nora closed her eyes to better concentrate. "What is an IHB?"

"An Investigator of Human Behavior. Our subgroup study is the investigation of nubile human female sexuality."

"Nubile human female sexuality..." Nora trailed off, confused.

"In easier terms, perhaps, it is the study of young, fertile human women and their response to sexual stimuli."

"But why us? We are obviously primitive compared to you." Nora was determined to get an answer.

"Primitive, yes, but still very beautiful."

Nora flushed under his enigmatic gaze. To her surprise, he reached one large hand under the blanket and found her thigh. Gently, he began to massage the muscles, first on the outside and then the inner thigh. The pleasure of his touch caught her off guard and she gasped. "You find us desirable?" she asked. Her throat felt suddenly dry.

"Desirable and interesting. You see, Nora, almost a half million years ago, we came from Earth. We looked very much like you, and we created a great civilization, but we almost destroyed ourselves with our uncontrolled technology. A passing stellar cloud of Phosinians—"

"Phosinians?" Nora interrupted.

"Phosinians are the EMTs of the universe. Because they travel naturally at the speed of light, they can respond quickly. They were passing as we were destroying ourselves and quickly moved us to Eluvia, a planet which orbits Alpha Centauri. Our star is twice the size of Earth. It is in the galaxy you humans call Centaurius."

To Nora's surprise, he suddenly stood up and came to her side. At just under nine feet tall, he towered over her. He was pure muscle and power. If he'd fought Dale Glower, the human would be a patch of bones in the ground. The angle of his face, the high cheekbones made him look almost human. Almost.

The red light in his middle eye dimmed slightly, but the blue eyes were piercing. He pulled down the sheet that covered her naked breasts and studied her with absorption.

She blushed beet red under his gaze. His large hands cupped her shoulders again. Slowly, he resumed his massage. His expression as he worked her body was intense, as if he were looking for something.

"You are lovely to look at and to touch," he answered, reading her mind again.

"You sound surprised," Nora said with a catch in her throat.

She had been watching him closely and saw his curiosity change to desire as he stroked her breast. It did something to her, too. She felt hotter and a little restless. She had to get back some control.

Then he moved to below her ribs and worked her rib cage. She sighed with pleasure. Under his absorbed gaze, she felt a sudden tingle between her legs.

"Why are you blushing?" he asked. She tried to pull up the sheet, but he gently brushed her hand away.

"You were telling me about the Eluvians?" she asked, trying to divert his attention.

He saw through her ploy, but he withdrew his hands and sat back down. Carefully, he recovered her under the blanket. It was a sensitive gesture that wasn't lost on Nora. Then he cleared his throat and began to explain everything to her. "As for the native Eluvians, they welcomed us, mated with us, and we became powerful in ourselves. Over the last five-hundred-thousand years, we have changed immensely as we adapted to our new world, but there is still a strong desire to understand what we once were.

"How much human DNA do you have?" she finally asked.

"Roughly ten to twenty percent, depending on the age of the Eluvian. For comparison, humans have about three percent Neanderthal DNA."

Nora's mouth felt dry and sticky. "Could I please have some water?'

Of course." The three eyed giant gently lifted her head and held a glass with a straw to her lips. She took a long swallow, then another one.

"Do you Eluvians drink water?"

"We hydrate but not like you." He took away the water.

"And you are here?"

"As I said, we are studying human female reproductivity. When we have completed our research, and we almost have, we will be beamed back to the mother ship. Then home."

"What if I don't want to participate?"

The Eluvian smiled. "You have no choice. I am master on this ship."

"And that makes me your slave?" Nora's blue eyes narrowed in indignation.

"I wouldn't call you my slave."

"What would you call it, Eluvian? A docile subject who has no power is a slave!"

"You are *not* a slave. You have freedom. When we are done, you will have even more freedom." He was getting annoyed at having to justify his work. "You will find your true self and you will act from courage, not fear."

Fear? Why did he say that?

"There is a lot of fear in you, Naughty Nora," he told her gravely.

She couldn't deny it. Fear of her father, fear of ex-husband, fear of life. There was silence, and it went on way too long. "I don't like it, but I have no choice, do I?" she mumbled.

"That's better." His lips twitched with what she suspected was almost a smile. But he was regarding her intently, as if considering something important.

What was he going to do to her? She shivered. He was so intense.

Then he reached down, lowered the blanket to her waist, and took her left nipple in his mouth.

"Oh, my goodness," she cried out, her little hands gripping his powerful arm right above his elbows. She felt his tongue flick over her nipple and suck a bit until she gasped with pleasure. His hot lips pulled away, pulling her nipple until she squeaked in surprise. He released her but kept his long fingers cupped around her breast. His mouth moved to the right nipple and his tongue circled the delicate skin around it until she moaned. Slowly, so slowly, he surrounded her orb with his mouth and repeated what he had done before. Nora felt a hotness between her legs that made her shift her hips back and forth. She was terrified but also incredibly aroused.

"What is your name… alien?" she asked in a whisper.

He didn't answer her question. His blue eyes pierced her thoughts. "I was just checking to see if you were still full of fire."

"I'm not. I'm frigid."

The alien made a low, laughing sound that argued his point better than words. "We will see about that, Naughty Nora."

"What do you mean?"

"You'll find out soon enough. Tomorrow, I think! We have already lost valuable time and our craft must return to the mother ship soon."

"Valuable time for what?"

He didn't answer. With one index finger, he reached out and, with infinite gentleness, traced a line from the corner of her mouth to her left breast.

"You may call me Eros until—"

"Until what?"

"Until you are prepared to call me Master!"

"That day will never come."

"Really?" He stepped back. "Don't be so sure. Someday, you may beg to call me Master. But for now, go to sleep."

"I don't want to sleep," Nora protested.

The alien again became stern. "You don't know what you want, Nora. You think you do, but you are like a child playing in the dark. And I must add, what you want ceased to become the crucial point when you entered this craft. I am master here, and you will do what I want! And right now, what I want is for you to sleep."

The large hand cupped her head and moved over her face, touching the diode in her scalp, and Nora felt herself sink into a sweet and dreamless sleep.

Chapter 3

Hours later, Nora opened her eyes and blinked with confusion. Where was she? Not home, of that she was sure! Her hand moved up to push back her hair and she felt the little metal sensor embedded in her scalp. Remembrance rushed into her mind, along with clarity.

She was on a spacecraft hovering above Earth. She was the captive of an attractive, but obviously dangerous alien who had saved her life, but who was now hinting at weird experiments. Eros was his name. She closed her eyes again and tried to lose herself in sleep, but after a few minutes she felt something brush her cheek. The sensation was so light that, at first, she thought she imagined it, but when it happened again, her eyes flew open.

Her heart stopped. What in heaven's name was she staring at? Or a better question was what creature was staring back at her? There was nothing in Nora's vocabulary or experience to classify the face peering at her intently.

The face and body were both a purple black, at least eight feet tall, and amazingly thin. Two yellow eyes, oval and intense, studied her. As with Eros, a red eye blinked between her eyes. There were two holes for a nose, and a long pink line Nora guessed was a mouth. The head was attached to a long neck the size of a broom handle that was attached to a chest no wider than the head, twelve inches at the widest point. Long, skinny arms and even longer legs were attached to the torso. If a praying mantis had mated with a bat, this would be their child. Like Eros, it wore a white lab coat.

The alien was the first to break the silence. "Good morning. I am Tria."

The staccato voice was familiar. It belonged to one of the aliens who had fixed her up when she was beamed aboard.

Nora managed to lick her lips enough to form words. "You scared me half to death. I think I just had a heart attack."

The alien took her words literally. Tria cocked her head and Nora noticed two knobs protruding from her scalp. They rose up four inches and turned toward Nora."

Tria waited one moment, then nodded, obviously satisfied. "No, you didn't. Your heart is fine."

She saw Nora's eyes move to her head and nodded. "These are my antennae. If needed, they expand upward."

Nora was slack-jawed with shock, but she managed to croak out a question. "You speak English?"

"I speak all human and all seven-thousand-seventy-seven living languages and dialects on Earth today and in nearby solar systems. I also am fluent in many dead languages, but that is not what you are asking."

"Who are you?"

"I just told you. I am Tria. I am Master Eros' assistant aboard this craft. I care for all the participants in the study along with other tasks. Please sit up now and swing your legs over the side of the bed." Tria patted the examination table near the bed. "Back up on the table, now. Master will be here soon."

"He's not my master," she mumbled rebelliously.

Tria ignored her and patted the top of the table. Nora counted seven fingers and no thumbs on her hand. Her feet were metallic and circular, like roller skates. When she moved, she glided across the floor.

It was pointless to argue with someone like Tria, Nora decided. She got off the bed and scurried to the table. Tria handed her a towel, and Nora wrapped herself in it. Feeling that it weakened her position, Nora didn't lie down. She sat, tense, her legs dangling over the side of the table.

"Does every craft have someone like you?" She spoke directly to Tria, who was reading something on what resembled a laptop.

"No. I stand alone. Three of the crafts have Roboticas. Your friend Jessie is on one of those. Robotica 712 is a full robot. They are efficient, but they lack life force intuition."

Nora simply didn't know what to say. She tried to act casual, failed, and then studied her hands. The manicure was perfect.

"Glad you like it," Tria said without looking up.

Damn! So Tria could read her mind, too! Well, Nora wasn't going to give her the satisfaction of complaining. Instead, she forced herself to stay calm. "Are you an Eluvian?"

"No. I am a Trieluvian." Tria cocked her head back and forth. "I was born on Eluvia, but my DNA profile shows that I am one third Trilota, one third Eluvian, and one third AI. Trilota is a moon that orbits around Eluvia."

"AI?"

"Artificial intelligence."

"Is that good?"

"Of course, it is good. If the Eluvians hadn't inserted AI into my DNA structure, I would be dead. I'm over fifty-thousand years old in human terms."

"And Eros?"

Tria looked past her and Nora jerked around. Eros strode

into the room smiling pleasantly. The lab coat was gone. Instead, he wore a black silky robe that came down to his knees. The Eluvian filled the space with his large presence and the force of his personality. He nodded to Nora and she clutched the blanket to her naked body.

"You want to know how old I am? In human terms?"

"Yes." Nora tried not to let her voice waiver.

Eros paced back and forth. "Hmm. Interesting calculation, but I guess I would be about twenty-thousand years old. That is pretty much the norm for my generation."

Nora studied him, saucer-eyed. "I can't imagine that!"

"Of course, you could if you had the right information. My essence has been reconstructed many times in the last twenty-thousand human years—"

"You've lost me? Essence?"

"We know how to replace parts so when one is not working properly, that part is replaced. You are starting to do that here on Earth with your primitive transplants. We've perfected it so that once every hundred years, we are reconstructed from top to bottom."

"Amazing." Nora couldn't hide her shock

"Yes, well, perhaps to you, but enough of that. I think I will update you and Tria right now," he said. "I just finished a conference with the mother ship. Eros Commander X has given me my instructions."

"Are you related?" Nora asked.

For once, both aliens were at a loss for words.

"Your name is Eros, and you said the commander is Eros Commander X." To Nora, it made sense.

"I see." Eros nodded. "Actually, I think Eros Commander X is a distant relation."

Tria nodded, too. "That is correct. This human is smart to have seen the connection. I will highlight this observation. Will we continue?"

Back to business.

"Of course. I must modify the sequences." Eros turned toward Nora and gave her his full attention.

"Nora, the study is created around a seven-day period. We study one human female for seven days and perform the prescribed experiments and note the data. Masters are allowed leeway to alter the experiments if there is a problem."

What happened to 'problems', she shuddered to think. Were they floating around space somewhere between here and the moon?

She gulped. "Am I a problem?'"

"Yes. But I have found a way to work around the time constraints. Since you were so badly injured, we have had to cut your time with us down to four days."

Four days! Nora's began to beat rapidly. *Four days of what?* She nodded, pretending she understood.

"Do you think she is up for it, Master? She has issues." Tria ignored Nora as if she weren't there.

"What issues?" What were they talking about?

Eros addressed Tria, "We don't have to do the exam. When we saved her life, we culled all the necessary information we needed."

"Correct," Tria agreed. "That is one day of work."

Nora tapped the table nervously to get their attention. "Wait a minute. What did you cull? What issues? I want some answers!"

Eros took her by the hand but still spoke to Tria. "I will use the shower experiment and that should do the trick."

"What trick?" Nora was really seething now. She didn't get angry often, but they were talking about her as if she were a lab specimen. Before she could say anything, Eros and his purple companion both finally turned and looked at her.

Tria spoke first. "But you *are* a lab specimen. We mean no harm by saying this."

It was too much for Nora. Suddenly, she couldn't take it anymore. She burst into tears. Wild, gulping sobs choked her throat.

She was a lab specimen. Dear Lord, how had it come to this? All she had ever wanted in life was a husband and children. Was that too much to ask? But instead, she had endured a horrible childhood, life with a dangerous and brutal husband, a near fatal car crash, and now, now, now, she had been abducted by aliens who looked on her as a lab specimen.

It was just all too much!

Chapter 4

Eros responded quickly to her tears. He took Nora into his powerful arms and held her tight. It was a protective and assured gesture. He knew what he was doing and didn't hesitate to take control.

"Tria, leave us," he commanded.

"But, Master, you will need—"

"Tria! Just turn on AI button red and record all information. It will be enough."

"If you are sure..." Tria sounded doubtful.

"I *am* sure, and I *am* master of this craft. This is how we will proceed. Is the shower ready?"

"Yes, of course." Tria quickly left. "But remember, no intercourse until tomorrow. She must heal."

To Nora's surprise, Eros tightened his grip and smoothed down her hair with his cheek. It was a soothing and oddly intimate motion that made Nora cry even harder.

"There, there, my little Naughty Nora. We were insensitive. You have been through so much. I am sorry."

Nora knew she was babbling, but she couldn't stop crying and talking through her tears. "First... endured a childhood ruined by my cruel father... insane husband, and now, I've been called... lab specimen? What the hell did that mean?"

"I know. I know. It has been tough for you. And for that very reason, I was overjoyed to get you as my last human. I think you will like what we will do next. It will calm you."

Eros spoke so calmly, so firmly, that it did calm her. He released her, pressed a button, and a panel slid open, revealing another room. He beckoned her to follow. Gently, he began to lead her toward the cubicle, but she balked.

"Come, Nora. You must trust me."

"No!"

Eros gripped her shoulders. His grip was light, but firm, and his tone brooked no argument. "You have no choice."

Gathering as much dignity as she could muster, she took two steps. Her head came to Eros's shoulder. "I am naked," Nora protested, clutching her blanket.

"So am I, under my robe." It was clear he was done with arguing. In one swift motion, he picked her up in powerful arms and carried her into the next cubicle. "We will shower together."

He set her on her feet and began to tap on a tile enclosed on the wall. Each time Eros touched the screen, a light flashed, showing signs that reminded Nora of hieroglyphics. She took the time to look around. Turning full circle, she saw there was no escape. They seemed to be sealed into this room that Nora guessed to be about six feet by six feet in dimension and three feet taller than the giant alien who was planning to give her a shower.

Oh, lord! How did this happen to her, she wondered in terrified, but awed confusion?

"There!" Eros turned to her with a satisfied nod.

Nora stared at him, wide-eyed. "Where is the shower?"

Eros laughed, putting his hands on her shoulders. He was so tall, she had to look up at him.

"We are in it. I was just adjusting the settings for our special enjoyment. Do you feel a soft, warm heat radiating over your body?"

"No." Nora quivered with apprehension.

"Maybe this will help."

Before she could object, he tore the blanket out of her hands and stepped back to gaze at her. Cowering back against the wall, she tried to protect her modesty and he laughed.

In response, she could only breathe heavier. And he was right. It was heating up in the cubicle. The floor under her feet was warming, and her body felt like it did when she was at the beach under a summer sun.

"Do you feel it now?" he asked softly.

"Yes. Yes, I do," she admitted. "As if I was getting a suntan."

"You *are* enjoying the healing of your sun. We have your sun's rays channeled into our heating system." He took a breath. "Do you smell the flowers?"

Nora inhaled. The lightest scent of roses teased her nostrils. Roses, lavender, and lilies, it was an intoxicating mix. She inhaled deeply. The effect on her senses made her feel a little lightheaded.

"Beautiful," she whispered. "And do I hear music?"

"Yes. I set it to very low, but it is a classical piece. Ode to Joy, I believe."

"Louder, please," she asked. "I love that piece."

"If I made it louder, it might distract us from our purpose in here. Just enjoy it as it is, like the faintest scent of flowers, the warmth of the sun, and the secure warmth of your native star."

Nora looked up at him in confusion.

"What is it?"

"But where is the water? If we are going to take a shower, then—"

Eros laughed and released her hands, stepping back. With one easy motion, he shrugged off his robe and stood before her totally naked. Naked and proud. He was magnificent.

Nora gasped. The lab coat had only hinted at his powerfully built frame. His chest and stomach rippled with muscles leading to thighs Nora had only seen on a mythical warrior. But it was his penis that made her catch her breath. He was huge. And he wasn't even erect. He smiled as he saw conflicting emotions cross her face—fear, followed by instinctive desire, then curiosity.

She looked up at him and met his teasing blue eyes. "It will never fit in me."

"Oh, but it will, little human woman. But not right now."

"The shower?" she asked.

"The shower, along with the examination." The playful Eros was gone. He was suddenly all business. "Are you ready?"

With one hand still covering her crotch, she looked around and then cried out as the room filled with moisture.

Hundreds of invisible jets began to release a cloud of moisture that pulsed into little bubbles. It wasn't water, but it was very warm and perfumed with a lemon scent she was unable to identify. The jets pulsed faster, and Nora felt she was getting a liquid massage. The moisture all over her body stimulated her skin. Whatever this stuff was, she loved it.

Eros had stepped back and watched with amusement as she played with the bubbles. Then he stepped forward and two large hands went around her waist, gripping her to his warm chest.

The intensity of the shower slowed and stopped. Now she could focus her attention on Eros.

"Did you enjoy the first part of your shower?" he murmured in her ear.

Instinctively, Nora froze. What was the right answer? Years of living with her crazy father and then her violent husband, made her cringe. She was so scared that nothing came to mind, not even yes or no.

She felt Eros's puzzlement in the slight loosening of his grip. "I asked you a question, Nora."

"Yes." She huddled into herself, heart pounding. "I heard you."

"I expect an answer." Curiosity getting the better of him, he then asked, "Are you frightened?"

"No! Yes! A little!" She blushed. "I don't know the right answer."

"Of course, you do. It was a simple question." He kissed the back of her neck with a gentleness that surprised her. "The right answer is the truth."

Nora gulped. How could she explain to this creature from another world how terrified she had been all her life? How could he possibly understand that even a simple yes or no could bring on a stinging blow of punishment.

He touched the red diode on her scalp and cursed. "Your fear is severe. Your reaction is that of someone who has been badly physically abused repeatedly, so often the body responds without conscious thought."

Eros turned toward the wall and spoke to someone other than Nora. "Human fear response. Taking action."

An examination table sprang out of the wall, and with one motion, Eros lifted Nora onto her stomach onto the table. Before she could react, invisible clamps locked her arms and legs into place. Eros was calm and efficient. It was clear to Nora that the aliens had seen this human response before and knew how to deal with it. That knowledge scared Nora even more.

"Please! Let me go home. I promise to—"

Eros interrupted her pleading with a nice pat to her fanny. "Record all my observations, Tria. I will send information through brain waves, not dialogue."

There was no response, but Eros seemed satisfied.

Eros patted her fanny again and leaned over her as he spoke close to her ear. "Today, my Naughty Nora, we are going to try some new things, to discover what excites a nubile human woman. But first, we must release the fear embedded in your body."

"No! Please! Let me go!" Nora struggled, but it was useless. She was locked into place. She blushed furiously, never having felt so naked. She could feel the alien's gaze on her body, and it was a sensation she could not describe. Hot, curious, ruthless. Eros had her completely in his power. He began by running his large hands through her hair and it fell around his wrists like strands of silk.

"I won't hurt you. I promise. Although a little pain might be stimulating."

Nora's heart sank. "I want to go home," she whispered, but the Eluvian shook his head.

"I promise you, Nora, that this will not be painful today. And as you heard, we have already done the examination part of the study. You were just unconscious, busy healing from your wounds, so you don't remember it. Today, we are combining two studies and doing the research to add to our conclusion. First, I will give you a massage designed to relax all your muscles.

As he leaned over her, she inhaled his scent, both masculine and wild.

"For all intents and purposes. It is just you and me in this room. Trust me. I am your master here. Are you going to call me Eros or Master?"

"Eros! No masters! Not safe for me," Nora cried out. "I'm naked and helpless."

"Then perhaps you should enjoy the release that brings."

"Release?" Nora spat out. She was acutely aware that she

was totally open to Eros's compelling gaze. "What are you going to do?" she cried out.

"For starters, I'm simply going to give you a massage and talk to you, tell you things, help you to relax." His giant hands began to knead her shoulders, gently at first, then harder.

"Lots of tension there," he remarked. "You carry it in your shoulders and back." His powerful hands were both gentle and demanding, and Nora felt the tension ease.

"You came all the way from space to give humans massages?"

The small room filled with Eros' laughter. "Oh, Nora! You have a good sense of humor!"

"I wasn't really joking," she huffed. She would have said more but his hands had found a particularly sensitive spot and she groaned with both pain and pleasure.

"You are still very tense."

"Considering the circumstances..." she trailed off. "What, actually, are you trying to discover?"

"Fair question. Eluvians are studying what arouses you, what responses you have to stimuli. It is the first part of our study of human reproduction. That study is down the road, but this will help us."

A deep, sharp pain in her shoulder blades made Nora groan. "That hurts."

"I imagine it does. Your muscles are unbelievably tight. That happens when you are exposed to a lot of stress." He pressed a spot halfway down her back by her lower rib cage and she gave out a little scream. "Right here. It is one of the tightest knots I've ever worked on."

"Why this massage?" Nora panted. She wanted to scream for him to stop but it also felt good. Releasing, in fact.

He moved to her waist and began to move her back and forth. There was something powerful about his touch that made her want to move her hips even more, but she tried to restrain herself. Then a thought occurred to her. As Eros moved down to her thighs, she debated asking him.

"I sense you have a question," he asked. When she didn't answer, he gave her buttocks a sharp slap. "I asked you a question. Do you want a spanking, Nora?"

She forced herself to turn her head to see him, then she decided to go for it. He was now working on her feet, and this was the closest to Heaven she had ever been. If she got him mad, and he killed her, she would at least die happy.

Another slap, half painful and half delicious. "Nora?"

"In step one, what did you find?"

"Pretty much just stress issues."

"Like my sore muscles."

"Oh, no. Far more serious." He moved to her buttocks and began to massage them. Nora was so embarrassed because he kept pulling her cheeks apart and, finally, with one hand, he began to circle her asshole slowly.

She thought she was going to die with embarrassment. "Please stop that. You are embarrassing me."

"Don't you like it?"

"No!"

"Liar. I see your breath rising." He pushed a little farther, and she squealed. "Ha, see!"

But he stopped, and then after a moment, she felt his fingers begin to renew his massage on her buttocks.

"What did you discover?"

"Your tests show that you have created stress hormones almost all your life. Do you ever wonder about your looks?"

"Looks?" Nora had his full attention. "What do you mean?"

"Well, your skin is so white, not because of pigmentation, but because you are anemic. You have a small, bleeding ulcer that Tria is now treating. It is too small for your doctor to easily find, but it was draining you."

She was shocked, but not really surprised. "That explains the stomach pains I get sometimes. What else?"

"Your hair is white-blonde and straight."

Nora smiled. "No surprise there. My mother was Swedish. I look like her."

"Ah, but you carry a gene, inherited from the female side, that has an odd reaction to stress. Your natural hair color is blonde, but a golden blonde, and it should be wavy, maybe even curly. The stress you and your mother lived under caused the color and curls to drain away."

Nora was so absorbed in thought that she didn't even notice when the Eluvian repositioned her. Suddenly, she was on her back. It was his sigh of pleasure that broke her train of thought and made her painfully and embarrassingly aware that she was stark naked and open to his gaze.

The Eluvian stepped back. "You are beautiful, my Naughty Nora. You are like a lush peach."

"Please, I…" she faltered, not sure of what she even wanted to say.

"I can see that you matured early. Your breasts are full and pink-tipped." Eros reached down and cupped her breasts, gently rotating them. "Very big. I like that in a young woman. And your nipples are pink and lush. Your hips are wide, for easy childbearing. You are not thin. I like that, too. You are a full woman and one of the best humans I have ever seen."

The Eluvian's voice had gone deeper, raspier. It was clear, he was aroused.

She opened her eyes a slit and saw that his cock was rising. Nora knew her face had gone scarlet under his perusal. The blush moved down her neck and to the top of her breasts.

"Why are you blushing? Are you aroused by my scrutiny?"

"A little," Nora admitted. "Actually, a lot."

He leaned in closer and cupped her breast. "Are you

remembering how I sucked on your nipple. It aroused you. I could tell."

Nora closed her eyes and shook her head. "No. No!" But her mind was recalling the power of his mouth against her breast.

"Don't worry. I won't hurt you. Quite the opposite, in fact."

The large hands began to massage her at her temples, moving in small circles around her scalp, behind her ears, and then again to the tense muscles of her neck. He worked slowly and with deliberation. Even though she wanted to dislike the alien touch, it was impossible.

After several minutes, those marvelous hands moved down to her rib cage, and then her hips, kneading and stroking, and in spite of herself, Nora began to relax. "Oh, that is so good." she whispered.

She was caught between wanting to cry from pain and then moan with pleasure. This wasn't lost on the Eluvian. The massage stopped for a moment. "I am going to press a little harder and it will hurt, but in the end, it will be for the best."

Eros didn't lie. He found spots that made her scream with pain when the kneading became too much. Tears rolled down her cheeks and he stopped to gently wipe them away.

"I'm sorry," she whispered.

"For what?"

"F-for crying."

"It is I who is sorry that to relax you, I must cause you pain." Eros was clearly startled.

"How did you know where to touch me?" Nora opened her eyes to see that he was carefully watching her.

"All researchers have to know the complete composition of the human body, each muscle, tendon, and nerve."

Again, his large hands encased her hips from the front and began to rotate and press and squeeze as she groaned with a new throbbing pleasure. He found muscles she didn't know she had that were sensitive and tight. And those muscles seemed to be connected deep in her womb.

"Very tight. I think you have moved throughout your whole life bound with apprehension."

"I guess tightening up made me feel protected."

To her surprise, the magic hands began to caress and knead the inside of her thighs. Bending each leg at the knee, the Eluvian alternated between legs, kneading the muscle and slowly stretched out her leg. This twisting and turning and massaging continued slowly. No rush!

"Protected from who? Your husband?"

Nora sighed. "Yes, later. But at first, I was scared of my father. He was a brute. He beat my mother and me when he drank."

"And yet you married a man just like him." The Eluvian's red light pulsed rapidly, recording this revelation. "This isn't the first time we have found this in humans."

"I didn't realize it at the time," Nora protested in self-defense.

"Humans seem to seek familiarity." Eros paused. "I think you have a saying, 'better the devil you know than the devil you don't'."

Nora bit her lower lip, thinking about his words. Could she possibly have married Dale because he was like her father? Ridiculous!

Eros went back to her breasts. "Yes. Very nice. Big, full. I like them."

"You sound like a human!"

He laughed. "Remember what I told you yesterday. Thousands and thousands of years ago, we came from Earth.

Nora was calm enough today to study him more closely. There was something very human about him. It was in the cheekbones and in the eyes.

"Primitive humans associated large breasts as similar to buttocks, and buttocks, of course, are very close to the vagina. Subconsciously, the association still exists."

Nora wasn't able to speak. All she could manage were short, shallow gulping breaths. Eros was still working on her breasts, kneading and squeezing, demanding something from her she was too afraid to understand. She gasped.

"Your mouth says no, but your body is saying yes." In response, one hand lifted and moved to her cunt, gently parting her lips and fondling her clit.

It felt exquisite, but she was so embarrassed at her response."

"Do you like that, my dear naughty girl?"

"No!" It came out strangled, hot with desire.

He moved a little closer and kept circling her clit, splaying her wide open so he could see her response. "But you like it. I can tell. You are so wet. Hot and wet, and very eager, Naughty Nora."

She closed her eyes and shook her head. But she was helpless under his touch.

"Your cunt has become very wet, very suddenly." Invisible fingers moved to the place where her ass met her thighs and edged inward.

Oh, why couldn't she stay calm and controlled? Why couldn't she just experience the moment and fling caution to the winds! The thought was immediately replaced by shame at the wild desire. What was happening to her?

"Do you like it?" asked. His voice had become gritty, hot.

"Oh, yes." She sniffed back a tear and tried to hide her response.

"What is wrong?"

"I am ashamed of my urges. My ex-husband said I was a whore."

"Your urges are normal, and your ex is a self-serving idiot!"

Nora was painfully aware that she was *so* naked to his sight and touch. Her breasts were flushed and her nipples hard. She could feel the Eluvian's scrutiny, and blood flooded her face. She lay there, naked and terrified. What was going to happen next?

"Why did you do this?" she cried out.

"Arouse you? It is the focus of our study."

"What are you going to do?"

The powerful hands again cupped her waist and then her rib cage, holding her gently, as if she was a great treasure. His tongue flicked back and forth over her nipples, clearly demanding a response.

Without meaning to do it, not even aware that she was arching her back, Nora groaned with pleasure. Eros traced a line from her breastbone to her pubic hair. The massage became gentle, cupping her hips, twisting and stroking her until she could respond with agility to a rhythm that was universal for all lovers.

"Ah. Very nice," he whispered hoarsely. "I think that when we mate, it will be a… very special for us both."

Powerful hands moved down to her thighs, gently pulling her legs apart even farther. Before she could even think, he parted her labia and slipped a large finger into her cunt.

Even though he was gentle, she sensed the power in his body. She wondered how he controlled that power as she took a deep breath. She cried out in fear, but desire, too. "You are so strong," she murmured.

"Does that scare you?" His voice was soft but commanding.

"It should," she breathed out, trying to form a coherent thought.

"Why?" Eros seemed genuinely puzzled. "Power is meant to arouse you."

"Power in a male means bruises and punches." She shook her head, trying to erase the memories.

His finger went higher, searching for something that she was instinctively eager to give him. If only she knew what it was! Nora felt her face glow red. This was way too intimate.

"Don't be shy," Eros whispered. "Show me how you feel."

"What are you going to do?" She didn't recognize her voice. It sounded so husky and wild. Nora had always hidden what she felt, and she tried to hide her passion now.

But the Eluvian was having nothing of that. "Part your legs more. The restraints will move with you. I want to see you. I want to see you when you come!"

"I won't come!"

"Our printout tells us that you are very intense emotionally and have high levels of stress hormones, even though you appear to be calm and controlled. The printout informs us that you have very high levels of hormones that usually decrease with orgasm. It is my opinion you have a lot of nervous energy because you are sexually frustrated."

There was a little slap on her thigh, but instead of being painful, the sting flooded her pussy with desire.

She tried to part her legs, but shyness inhibited her. Her attempts weren't enough for Eros. Powerful hands that would not be denied pulled her thighs farther apart, leaving her completely exposed. "Don't you want to know what I see?" Eros asked her softly. "Show me! Show me. You are close."

"No," she gasped. "No!"

"Liar. Your breathing has become so ragged."

Nora's eyes were jammed closed. She felt on fire under his intense scrutiny. He was studying every part of her most intimate spots.

"Nice." His other hand moved to her clit.

With one finger in her cunt and another massaging her clit, she was starting to lose control. She bucked upward, then down, then up again. His fingers were playing her like a violin. He wanted to see her lose control and he would not be denied.

Eros was relentless. Nora could feel a pressure in her vagina. There was a stroking, so slowly, she wanted... she didn't know what she wanted. She was so wet.

"When did you lose your virginity?" he whispered huskily.

She could barely speak under his relentless touch. "On my wedding night. I was seventeen. Dale and I eloped."

She felt a pressure, hot and wild. "How many lovers?"

"Only Dale."

"Don't lie."

"I'm not!" she gasped.

"You are very tight. Almost like a virgin. You have not been stretched out by a man's penis."

His finger was bigger than Dale's penis. Goodness, this was crazy. She couldn't stop moving with his rhythm.

"What is happening? Help me!" she screamed out.

Eros was gentle but never broke his rhythm.

When Nora didn't answer, he continued. "Have you ever climaxed before, Naughty Nora?"

"Yes. I guess. It was... not much. Like a pleasant sneeze."

Eros shouted out a cry of laughter and moved his finger faster. Her hand restraints were gone, and she thrust upward, not able to stop. She was mortified, aroused, confused. But nothing could stop her body from following his lead.

"What is happening?" she screamed. "What are you doing to me?"

To her embarrassment and chagrin, the large hand slowly moved out, cupped her clit and stroked her until she was pleading for mercy.

"Tell me you need it!" the Eluvian demanded in a fierce

whisper that was more like a hiss. "Tell me. Tell me. I won't bring you to the peak until you say it! "

She was floundering and she knew it.

"Tell me, Nora! I command you! Your big breasts are shaking with desire."

"I want—" Face flushed red, she struggled with the words. She could barely control her excitement.

"Beg me." It was almost a command she had to obey.

"I want to come!" she screamed. Without realizing it, she began to pound her fists against his chest, gasping for a release that demanded she beg for mercy.

The finger moved even higher and found a spot that made her arch and scream with pleasure.

"There. I found it," he yelled in triumph. He stroked with abandon, and she went higher, higher, higher, and then exploded, over the edge of delight, into mind-numbing ecstasy.

Did she pass out?

As she lay half-conscious on the table, she suddenly felt the warmth of the Eluvian shower descend on her naked body. Then she felt Eros' hands, heavily lathered, begin to wash her hair. He worked slowly, with measured and careful strokes, massaging her scalp. Then he rinsed her hair and began on her neck. The hard massage was gone. His hands were now working her body with caresses too wonderful to stop.

She gave a deep sigh when he reached her arms, breasts, her waist, then her thigh, calves, and feet. Then he moved to her pussy and began to lather her there, parting her legs and soaping her labia, her vagina, and her ass. She opened her eyes like a woman drugged and saw his own blue eye, usually flashing sparks, strangely calm.

He saw her looking at him, and he gave her a sheepish grin. "You have mesmerized me, Naughty Nora. Like no other human has done before."

She closed her eyes, not sure what he meant. He stepped back and she was rinsed clean by a hot shower that made her tingle.

Then he picked her up and dried her off in his robe and carried her back to the sleeping cubicle.

He stayed with her for a long time as she rested. "You contracted so violently that I feared for my finger," he whispered. "I can't wait until we make love together. Wait until you feel my enormous cock in your pussy!"

His hot breath on her skin made her body tingle. As she lay on the bed half-conscious, he carefully wrapped her up in a warm blanket.

"Rest now, my dear. Tria will check on you later."

Chapter 5

The hours after Eros left her were a blur in her mind. She was totally exhausted and yet she felt wonderful. She slipped into a deep sleep that was filled with dreams of warm blue sea and waves lapping the sand of a coral beach. He had done things to her that she never expected, never even knew could happen.

She awoke to the sounds of Tria bustling like a gigantic moth around her. She half opened one eye and saw the tiny little orbs that were Tria's feet bouncing off the floor.

Tria caught her staring but didn't comment. "Put on your robe and come over to the table I have set. I have all your favorite foods for your lunch. Swedish pancakes, crisp bacon, coffee.

Nora realized she was starving. She was up in a flash and suddenly felt lightheaded.

Tria supported her with one thin arm that, surprisingly, had steely strength. "Careful. You have gone through so many sensations, plus, you are still healing. I told my master not to bring you to orgasm, but he said he couldn't help himself."

Nora blushed red, suddenly remembering that Tria had

knowledge of the entire encounter. She sank into the chair at the table and inhaled the coffee with cream and sugar.

"Butter and hot maple syrup?" Tria fluttered over to the table and offered more food.

"Oh, yes! I don't remember when I was this hungry."

"It is the good sex. He is very good, my master."

Nora put down her fork and met Tria's golden gaze. "Were you aware the whole time?"

"What do you mean?"

"Did you… see… what he did to me?"

Tria's red eye flickered. It was clear she was trying to understand what Nora was asking and choosing her response carefully. "I think my master explained it all to you. Before your shower, I went into 'record and document' mode. To do that, I set my position to AI. I could see and hear, but there was no emotion or recognition. Do you understand?"

"A little, but it is hard," Nora admitted. She lifted a slice of bacon to her mouth and took a bite. It was perfect, the best she had ever tasted. She told Tria, who just nodded, and asked, "Where did you get your training?"

"In what? I am trained in many things."

"Cooking, research, languages?" Nora tossed out as many ideas as first came to her.

"After my training in languages, I decided to enter the research and exploration service in support services. They trained me to support a science master in any way he or she would deem necessary."

"Have you been on different projects?"

"Yes. But this is the longest one I have been involved with. Master Eros asked for me specifically because we worked together on comet exploration. We are a good match."

Nora nodded and took a sip of coffee. Again, perfect.

"How do you know what humans like? You are spot on, as they say."

Tria pulled out a tray of capsules and began to organize them. "Eluvians have been studying humans for at least forty-thousand years. For a while, we thought the Neanderthals were going to win out, but your group prevailed. That study was on food creation, like farming and hunting prey."

"When did you shift to this study?"

Tria thought for a moment, her red light calculating. "Sorry. I'm not as young as I used to be, or as quick. Remembering back forty-thousand years takes a second. I started with a different master, but I didn't like him, so I left and went to the Saturn ring study. Interesting."

Nora was thoughtful. "There is a big debate on Earth about aliens. But now I see that you have been watching us for a long time."

Tria nodded confirmation. "This has been a long study, and you and your friends are the last to be examined. The tests are the same, but masters can change some things. Our master, Eros, asked for me specifically. I can deny him nothing. He is too good at what he does."

Nora's eyes widened. What, exactly, did that mean? But she had learned something in the last few days and that was to not ask too many questions. If it didn't concern her, then let it go.

Tria nodded in assent and tossed the pill containers into different bins.

Also, Nora had something else to think about. Her closest friends were all undergoing the same experience. Wow. Gilly would probably be fine. And Jessie, too. But shy, timid Rose was a virgin raised by a strict, religious aunt. Would she survive this experience?

She looked up and swore that Tria was grinning at her.

"What?"

"Oh, nothing. You'll find out. Someday."

"Find out what?" Nora demanded. When it came to her

friends, she could be protective. "Are they okay? My friends, I. mean."

"More than okay. I read their information on the computer." Tria paused, considering her words carefully. "Your friend Jessie is on a craft where the master conducts the experiments under the cloak of invisibility. My master, Eros, prefers to be visible to the subject."

"I'm glad."

"This is my last trip."

Nora stared at the alien. Did she mean she was dying? How could you tell when the living object looked like Tria? Eight feet tall, purple-black, and as wide as a ruler, not to mention the three eyes and two antennae.

Tria seemed to read her mind. "I'm fine. But the study is ending, and I want new adventures. I want to fly all over the universe and see new things."

Involuntarily, Nora looked down at Tria's tiny feet. Was she hovering or standing? "Can you fly by yourself?"

Tria shrugged. "Of course. I can fly at about five-hundred miles an hour as you record it on Earth, but to fly from galaxy to galaxy takes planning. I will have to go on a spacecraft. It is a little hard to find one with an empty seat."

Something came to Nora's mind and she debated for only one moment. "You have been alive many years."

"Earth time." Tria nodded.

"So, do you ever die?"

"When we choose to cease functioning, we can evolve into pure energy."

"My mother died. Five years ago."

"Nothing dies. It just changes form. If your mother left her body here on Earth, she is somewhere else, in another form."

"What form?" Nora couldn't keep the anguish out of her voice. Her mother had been her world. She never would have married Dale if her mother had lived. But she had been so lonely, and he needed her love. Or so she thought! He was lonely because he was a bastard and a brute.

Tria shook her head. "There is no way I can tell, my dear. She might be a beam of light or a sentient creature. Only the higher forces know where each living thing goes."

Nora almost cried at the sound of kindness in the alien's voice. But she felt a lot better. Without speaking, she ate all her food and got seconds on the coffee. Both she and Tria were silent for the rest of the meal, but when Tria went to leave, Nora spoke up. "Tria?"

"I refuse to call any man master." Nora felt she had to make this clear. "After what I've been through in my life, I call no man master."

Tria's gaze was enigmatic. "That may be true. But Eros is not a man, is he?"

Nora couldn't think of a response. She sat alone in the empty room, sipping what remained of her coffee and trying to work things out in her head.

Chapter 6

L ater in the day, Eros came to see her. She blushed red, remembering the intimacy they had shared, but he seemed to be all business.

Was it possible she had imagined his soft words before he left her? An upsetting thought came to her. Perhaps that intimacy was part of the experiment. Before she could ask any questions and shame herself by showing neediness, she noticed he was setting up a round crystal object, a little larger than a basketball.

"Come over here. I have something to show you," he commanded.

Nora had slipped into a long blue nightgown made of something shimmery, almost transparent. But the material still managed to keep her warm and was comforting.

She went over to the table and watched curiously, as Eros punched in numbers on a part of the object that appeared to have dots in all numerations on it.

"What is it?" she asked.

"This is a CCIB?"

"What?"

"A craft connection information board. I am connecting you with the mother ship. I think you might want to see this."

Nora leaned closer and laughed with delight when she saw the screen. Muffin was wagging his tail and playing with a ball.

"Oh, thank you, thank you. Is his leg in a cast?"

Eros peered at the screen. "Yes. It was broken in two places, but he will be fine. In a few days, the cast should come off. He has been given advance healing solutions."

"Muffin, Muffin, it's me, Mommy," Nora cried into the screen, but the dog gave no indication he heard her.

"Can he see me? And wait. What is that thing between his eyes?"

"He can't see you. It was decided he would get too excited. And that spot is a sensor, just like you have. He is communicating quite well with one of our staff who is sensitive to dog brain waves. Evidently, he is quite interested in music."

Nora stared at Eros, completely baffled. "I know Muffin communicates with me. He tells me he is hungry, sad, tired. But music? Isn't that impossible?""

"Not at all. You humans are so self-centered. It is your greatest flaw. If a life form can't communicate in human terms, like speech or hand signals, you consider that life form inferior. But that is not true. Muffin loves music. I was told he is partial to Beethoven."

"When I return to Earth, I will get a piano when I can afford it. I used to play when I was young. Maybe he will like that."

Eros continued to stare at her, his expression enigmatic. Nora turned back to the screen, but the image flickered, and the screen went dark.

She sighed. "Goodness! I miss him so much. He and my friends are my whole family now."

He was still silent, still studying her. His blue eyes flashed sparks. She eyed him with apprehension. What was going to happen?

Trying to fake a calmness she didn't feel, she ironed out a crease in her gown. "Tria gave me the gown. She said it was made of Galinta thread."

"Very pretty. Tria has good taste. She is very artistic."

"You're kidding?" Nora laughed.

Eros pulled up a bench. "That shade of blue suits you, and I'm very happy to see that your color is better. There is a faint blush to your cheeks, and at the nape of your neck, I see a tiny curl. It is shy, just like you."

Involuntarily, Nora's hand flew to her face. Her skin felt warm.

"Is it because I am gazing at you?"

Nora blushed. He was right, but she didn't want to admit it. There was a light in his gaze that always made her warm. It was as if there was a fire within that made him warm to the touch.

"I asked you a question. If you don't answer, I will have to punish you."

That got her attention. "Yes! Yes! It makes me… shy when you look at me with that certain look."

"That certain look? I think you mean desire, Naughty Nora." His voice grew lower. "Tomorrow, we will make love."

"But—" Nora was at a loss for words.

"But nothing, my dear Naughty Nora. I just want you to anticipate our coupling. And tonight, I want to give you something that will make it easier."

"Easier?" Her blue eyes grew wide with concern and curiosity.

"I am very big."

"I'm not a virgin," she protested, but he just got up and left the room. She was left alone with the CCIB, left alone and completely confused.

Chapter 7

In spite of herself, Nora fell asleep on the bed, sinking into a delightful little nap. For years, her dreams had been plagued by nightmares, but today, she had a dream in which she was totally happy. No dark shadow of violence darkened the room. In it, she was a young woman, an age her mother had never had a chance to see. They were making Christmas cookies. It was a recipe from Sweden, and Nora's job was to cut the cookies with a cutter. Her mother was so proud of her.

"Naughty Nora." Her mother laughed. "Here you are, a grown woman and I will bet you will steal a few cookies!"

Nora never wanted to wake up. When something nipped at her toe, she pushed it away with irritation. The distraction landed on her chest with a leap and began to lick her face. This got her attention. Somehow, was Muffin back? For Muffin, she would wake up.

Her eyes flew open.

Dear lord! What was it staring her in the face, two inches from her nose?

It was a ball of white fur the size of a soccer ball. Beneath four flappy ears, four red eyes stared back at her, and a long red straw flashed out of its mouth and licked her face. Before she could utter a sound, Tria came into the room and began to bustle around on those little ball feet. Her antennae were retracted, and she wore a bright red lab coat. Instead of a bat, she now resembled a colorful moth.

"I see that Borgo likes you," she observed. "Why don't you come sit over at the table? I have a drink of this fruit juice and some cookies. Your readings tell me you are dehydrated. Not surprising, considering your exertions earlier in the day.

"What is… it?" Nora asked. Borgo seemed really friendly, but she couldn't even identify what it was.

Tria came over and lifted Borgo off Nora and brought it to the table. She sat down and cuddled Borgo. Nora sprang up and went to the table.

"Borgo is my pet. I see Master has shown you Muffin," Tria said, pouring the juice into a glass with one hand.

They both looked at the CCIB.

But curiosity overcame Nora. "Is Borgo a cat, a dog, a rabbit?"

"None of them. Borgo is a member of the Borgogian from the comet Partarpa. They are hatched, like birds, but are warm-blooded. We harvest their eggs from the comet when it passes by Eluvia once every thousand years.

"May I hold him? Her?"

"Neither. Borgo is sexless."

Nora reached out and petted Borgo's silky white fur. Borgo couldn't weigh more than six pounds, she thought.

"Four eyes, four ears. Does it have four legs?"

"Six. Two can also be used as wings." Tria nodded proudly. "I love Borgo."

Nora studied the purple face so tenderly cradling her little pet.

"I understand. Muffin is my family, too. He's all I've got. Except for my three best friends."

"No sisters or brothers?"

"Both my parents were only children, and I was an only child. Now that my mother is dead and my father has disappeared, it's just me and Muffin and the girls."

Tria studied Nora. "You aren't telling me everything."

Nora thought about the note. "Well, my father has suddenly reappeared. He left a note for me, but you and Eros captured me before I was forced to see him." Nora's eyes were bright with unshed tears. "What about you?"

"My cluster, or family, as you call it, has approximately two-thousand members. We were raised together in a laboratory setting and then given our choices of assignments. Sometimes I run into a fellow sibling, but the universe is vast. I chose to go into research. Master Eros and I are compatible. He appreciates my efficiency and my insights. I think of him as my family, too."

"Will you miss him when this study is over?"

The answer surprised Nora. It was an emphatic no!

"Eros and I will always keep in touch, but I want to do something different and develop another side to my personalities.

Nora caught the plural. "How many personalities do you have?"

"Many. You see, being made of three different life forms, I can have more options than, say, you."

Nora took a sip of the drink and frowned. "Does Eros know?"

"About my multiple personalities?"

"No. About your desire to change work."

"Of course, he knows. He thinks it is a wonderful idea. He and Eros Commander X want me to take an assignment on Earth making contact with Earth bats. In the universal community, Trieluvians are known as the bat creatures because of our strong resemblance to Earth bats. When we mated with Eluvians, we grew taller and thinner, and this is the result. Quite nice, I think."

Nora put down her cup and studied Tria. Over six feet tall, no more than twelve inches wide, purple-black with two antennae, and ball bearings for feet, not to mention three eyes, yet she was quite pretty. She had a shining quality to her.

"I think you are lovely," Nora said honestly. "A week ago, I would have seen you with different eyes, but now I can see your beauty."

"Very good. You are expanding your mind."

Borgo yelped and Tria cuddled him. "He is hungry. Time for his milk."

Nora looked on with fascination as Tria took out a bowl and poured milk into it.

She set Borgo loose as the little creature opened his mouth and a straw appeared where the tongue had been. Borgo drank all the milk through the straw mouth, then settled down immediately and fell asleep.

"Would a Borgo survive on earth?" Nora asked with curiosity.

Tria gave her an odd look, as if she was debating something. The narrow shoulders went up in a shrug. "We both would. We were reprogrammed a few centuries back to do reconnaissance work on Earth."

"Spying on humans?"

"Yes." Tria's red eye blinked faster as she recalled her experience. "I almost got burned at the stake. Someone spotted Borgo and me transporting quickly through the air and the village came running with pitchforks!"

"You're kidding!"

"Kidding is not a natural trait for me," Tria responded tartly. "I only tell the truth."

"Oh, my goodness. They thought you were a witch." Nora couldn't control her laughter. She could just imagine the terrified villagers spotting purple-black, six-foot high, twelve-inch wide, three-eyed Tria over the village square! "Where was this?"

"Some place called Romania. Of course, Borgo and I just disappeared, but it had terrible consequences." Tria's antennae quivered at the memory.

"But you said you escaped?"

"Of course. Beings of the higher power can disappear at will. We were fine. But the ignorant villagers needed to assuage their fear and they decided the real witch was a poor old woman who lived on the outskirts of town. They burned *her* at the stake instead."

The terrible story wiped the laughter form Nora's face. "That was awful. Couldn't you have stopped it?"

"I was long gone. I heard about it many years later and I have always felt guilty that I allowed myself to be seen by primitive humans."

"Things have changed," Nora tried to comfort her.

"Have they?" Tria looked doubtful. "Violent solutions are not the answer to problems and fears, and that is still something humans need to really embrace. Your ex-husband is a perfect example."

Tria, who looked like a demented moth/bat, was wiser and kinder than many people she knew.

Eros returned just as she was readying for bed.

"Why are you here?" Nora asked.

"To see you, of course," Eros replied. He knelt down at her feet.

His warm, large hands shifted to her knees, massaging her

legs through the material. With one slow motion, he pushed her gown up to her waist. She flushed bright red under his knowing gaze. With infinite gentleness, he leaned down and kissed her pussy, blowing gently on the folds of her skin until she squirmed with a flash of his fire. Slowly, slowly, he parted her thighs until she was spread wide open to his gaze.

He smiled and took a little bottle out of his pocket, uncapping it. "You may not be a virgin, Naughty Nora, but you are very tight. And I am very big, and when we make love, I will swell even larger. I want our coupling to be sexy for you. This lotion will soften you through the night and make it easier for you to take all of me into your cunt."

Nora swallowed hard as he gently parted her labia, searching for the entrance to her most private spot. Her legs trembled in fear and desire as she felt him press his finger inside her, looking for the best place to put the lotion. He removed his hand and then immediately replaced his finger with the tip of the bottle and squeezed. It was something hot and creamy and it flooded her vagina.

Then, with a smile, he stood up and smiled. "There. That should help."

She couldn't help it. "You are going to leave me like this?" she cried. Shamed by her own desire, her breath grew rapid.

"I must. It would not be good to do anything more right now. I want to keep you safe."

She looked up at him, trembling even more. "I know I am shameful, but I saw how big you are. I want you now."

"Nora—"

"I need you now!"

"You are not ready. I realized that today. You must be made ready. When I am aroused, I will swell even larger."

"Just how big are you?

He smiled, his blue eyes flashing right into her eyes.

"You'll find out."

Chapter 8

Perhaps it was the anticipation of the day to come, or the knowledge that the oil inside her was preparing her for intercourse with Eros, but her sleep was light and broken with dreams. The warm oil inside her vagina made her squirm with anticipation. She could almost feel her vagina soften in preparation for lovemaking. Finally, when she thought she would not sleep at all, she fell into a deep slumber. She awoke refreshed, rested, and anxious, all at the same time.

After another fantastic shower, Tria stood ready to prepare her for the next experiment. She held up an identical gown to the one she had worn yesterday. The Trieluvian was thoughtful. "He asked that you wear this particular dress. He has never done that before," Tria mused as she brushed Nora's hair.

"He said he liked me in it," Nora offered.

Tria rolled back and studied Nora. "That is what is worrying me. First, your friend Jessie caused problems. Now my master is acting oddly. He has never done that before. I hope, now, on the last study, we don't have problems."

Nora's ears perked up immediately at the mention of Jessie. "What kind of problems?"

From the interested expression on Nora's face, Tria realized she had said too much. She took a step back. "Nothing for you to concern yourself with. All I'm saying is that you and your friends are more of a handful than we had anticipated. Anyway, I am the one who reports to the mother ship if anything is amiss."

There was a lot to think about in that statement, but before Nora could ask anything else, Eros entered the room and waved to Tria.

"On auto robot, please." Eros' command was brisk and take charge.

Tria moved quickly across the floor and went rigid.

"She looks like a bat when she does that," Nora couldn't help observing.

Eros half glanced at Tria but didn't comment.

Nora studied him. Did he come in here to discuss the creature on the wall?

Instinctively, she recognized in his pacing that he was debating something. She wasn't wrong.

Eros strode over to her and lifted her up in his powerful arms. Her brutal ex-husband was tall, but Eros had him beat by almost three feet. And there was no contest in the strength department. His red eye blinked at her and he sat down on the couch, cradling her in his arms.

"Do you know what Eros means?"

"Is it the root word for erotic?"

"Very good." One large finger moved through her hair and then traced a thin line over her cheek, down her neck, and under the sheer negligee. His lips found the curl at the nape of her neck and began to kiss her. Instinctively, she arched her back at his touch and closed her eyes. His thumb found her right nipple and made very light circles around it.

Nora took a deep breath and tried to settle herself. His kisses were too delightful.

"Eros was the god of sexual love in ancient Greek mythology. My actual name is a numerical construction that would mean nothing to humans, but some of us took names that humans could relate to."

"Eros," Nora whispered.

"It sounds so sexy when you say it," he murmured, and his finger came back and traced the outline of her lips. "I want to explain a little more of this study to you so you can better understand."

"Then you'd better stop kissing me like that." Nora spoke frankly.

He laughed and stopped, but he kept her positioned on his lap. "The rules of the study are clear. It lasts five to seven days. We are ordered to conduct a certain number of experiments on our human subjects and a recommendation on how to proceed. But the final decision is left to the master of each craft. Three tests are non-negotiable. We must do a complete examination of your body, perform oral sex on you, and we must have intercourse."

"You have only done one of those," Nora whispered. "We haven't had intercourse and you haven't performed oral sex on me."

"Right. But listen. The other three tests are you performing oral sex on me, a threesome, and anal sex. I am at liberty to drop one of those.

Nora flushed. "I don't think I want the last one. Anal, I mean."

"Good, because we have started to run out of time. Because of your injuries, we lost two days. And once again, I have changed the order of the study chapters."

"I don't understand?" Nora tried to breath normally, but she was acutely aware that a certain part of Eros was growing large under her lap. If he was going to insert his penis in her now, she wasn't sure she would be able to take all of him inside her body. In spite of herself, her hips began to rock back and forth.

"Once again, I have decided to change the order. I feel you need a little more time for the more... stressful parts of the experiments."

Before Nora could comment about this, one of the panels slid open and a creature dressed all in white entered the room. He looked very human, and yet he didn't. His skin and hair were as white as his suit, but his two blue eyes were silvery. Suddenly, she remembered the man by the side of the road who had directed Jessie to take the forest road. Why was he here?

"This is my colleague, Observer 21270-p. You may call him Obe if you like."

"Why should I be calling him anything?" Nora asked, her lower lip trembling with sudden fear.

"I'll explain."

"He is human," Jessie protested weakly.

The creature with hair the color of snow smiled and nodded in her direction. "I am pleased that you find me to be a human. Thank you."

"Sit down, Obe," Eros commanded. He turned back to Nora. "Obe is one of my kind but has been outfitted in a suit that makes him look human. His job is to observe and report back about activities on Earth. It is a first rung position in our exploration system. I did it in my youth. I was assigned to ancient Britannia. I didn't care for it too much. The natives were preoccupied with moving stones from one place to another."

Obe nodded. "I believe you are referring to a place called Stonehenge."

Eros laughed. "I got so sick of watching them, I levitated

four of the giant stones to their present location just to get them to do something else."

"Did they?"

"Actually, no. They got even more fired up. I went back to check it out and was amazed at the hundreds of tourists who come each day."

Eros was stalling and Nora knew it. She threw her head back and took a deep breath. "What is going on? Why is the Observer here?"

Obe patted her knee, then he took her right hand. Like Eros, he was surprisingly warm. "We didn't find you by accident. I have been living in your area for a while, sizing up the situation."

"So I've been told, by Eros. What do you have to do with it?"

Eros gave her a little hug. "When you return to your world, Obe will be there if you have any problems."

It was clear Eros was choosing his words carefully. "I want him to observe you in the act of sex so that the intimacy between you both can be greater."

"But I don't want intimacy! I don't want to be observed in a moment of intimacy. I want…"

"What?"

Nora opened her mouth to speak, but she couldn't say a word. She didn't know what she wanted. Eros had been right to tell her that. Both he and Obe didn't seem surprised at her confusion. Obe stood up and moved before her. The lights dimmed as he slowly stripped off his clothes, first his white shirt, and then his blue jeans. He wore nothing underneath.

Nora watched him, spellbound. Dressed, Obe seemed a little odd, but naked, he was very sexy. He leaned toward her. His hands were strong but gentle as he held her close.

"Don't be afraid," Obe whispered in her ear. "We won't hurt you."

When she didn't answer, he spoke again. "I am naked now."

"Yes, you are," she whispered, a catch in her throat.

"My human suit is built just like a human male." He encouraged her by taking her hand and fondling his balls.

"Oh, my!" she cried out, but she realized she didn't know what she was saying.

"Oh, my, what?" This was from Eros, a low, musical sound, but still, definitely a command.

"Pay attention to me, now! Let us please you," Eros whispered. He was at her feet, and Obe moved behind the bed and put his hands on her neck.

"What are you going to do?" Her voice trembled with excitement.

"Reach out and touch Obe. His manhood is straining toward you like a flower to the sun."

Nora obeyed, taking Obe into her little hands and stroking him. Even though he was not as big as Eros, he was still huge compared to a human male. The alien groaned out his delight at her touch.

Eros reached out and brushed a wavy strand of hair from her face. "We will find great pleasure, the three of us. This is our threesome and I think you will enjoy it very much."

"Is that a command or a promise?" Nora gasped, trying to steady herself.

"Both."

Eros's hands moved again to the ribbons, and with one gentle pull, the negligee opened, revealing Nora's naked body. Nora clutched his hands, suddenly, unbearably embarrassed and shy. Obe reached out and grabbed her little hands and Eros peeled the silky material from her body.

"Very nice. You are still very pale, but now there is a pink sheen to your body. Even if it is only your blush of embarrassment, it is still very nice."

"Very nice," Obe agreed. "Like a marble statue come to life."

"You will like this," Eros promised, smiling at her as his he parted her legs and positioned her perfectly for his gaze. "Close your eyes."

When she didn't obey, he was stern. "If you don't obey, I will have to spank you. Or better yet, I will have Obe spank you."

The idea was so arousing that Nora gasped. She jammed her eyes shut and blushed red over her throat. The flush moved over down onto her breasts. In spite of her determination not to respond, she was getting excited and showing her arousal. She inhaled, trying to breathe normally but failed completely. What was going to happen?

Obe's hands moved over her breasts, just as Eros began to kiss the inside of her thighs.

Oh, my! Oh, my!

His tongue followed his hands from her thighs to her pubic hair in agonizing slowness. And then she felt him, felt him tease her pussy with his lips and then his tongue. "You can open your eyes and watch," he whispered, his voice hoarse with desire.

Her lids rose and she took him in, between her naked legs, licking her pussy with a red tongue that looked remarkably human. With every flick, he moved closer to her clitoris, and she realized that this was the ultimate tantalizing dance of desire.

Obe's lips found her neck and he began to pepper her with soft kisses as he cupped her straining breasts. She couldn't hold back a moan of pleasure.

Eros smiled. He ran his finger between her legs and nodded. "You are so wet, Nora. I have seen few humans respond like you do."

"Oh, my goodness," she screamed. "I can't believe this. I'm a good girl! I'm not really naughty!"

In response, both Eros and Obe laughed.

Eros, on his knees, was so big that his head was still higher than hers.

She was openly naked to the gaze of the men—totally naked. Her feeble attempts to protect herself had no effect on the Eluvians.

Without any effort at all, Obe, still behind her, lifted her up and placed her face down over Eros' lap. Eros' huge cock pushed into her breasts. With one hand, he held her in place.

"Nora! You can't fight us. You must trust us." Eros was totally in command. There was something in the way he spoke that calmed her for one moment, and her rapid breathing slowed.

"Don't be frightened or shy. Today, I will only give you pleasure and Obe will assist."

"How?"

Obe moved from behind the couch and positioned himself over her. His hands, smaller than Eros' large ones, were hot. He inserted one finger between her legs and gently rubbed her most delicate private parts. She was so wet that his finger slithered across her skin. His touch made Nora want to cry out with pleasure.

"What do you find?" Eros asked with a catch in his throat.

"She is dripping with desire. May I take her now?"

"Yes, but don't let her come."

With one movement, Obe knelt over her body and put his hands around her waist. "Don't worry, Nora," he whispered. "I will be careful, and I will be fast. I can tell you will satisfy me quickly."

Then, Obe parted her legs from behind and, with one slow motion, positioned his cock in her pussy, slowly pushing his cock at the mouth of her vagina. With a low, exquisite thrust, he moved inside her and began to rock back and forth.

The pleasure that Nora felt was so exquisite that a groan escaped her lips, a ragged sigh of carnality. Her hips rose up involuntarily. That involuntary motion of hers was what Obe had been waiting for.

"See. Nothing is hurting you," he whispered huskily as he parted her legs even more.

"She is so close to coming," he whispered, "I must come quickly and then release her."

Stroke, stroke, stroke.

He lifted her hips for each plunge into her most private parts, and Nora could feel his excitement growing. She was so close, she wanted to buck and scream for release, but with superhuman control, Obe wouldn't let her come, instead concentrating on his own pleasure. This was wildly exciting, his control and his movements.

Stroke, stroke, stroke, and then… he bucked high, lifting right off the couch, as he came within her.

"Ahh," he cried out then fell on top of her.

Nora wanted to scream with frustration, but before she could say or do anything, Obe was up and washing her off. He had worn a condom so there was little to do before Eros again flipped her and she was back where she had started, upright, legs splayed open, Obe's hands on her shoulders. And she was totally open to their gaze. Nothing was hidden.

Except now, her cheeks were flushed dusty red, her eyes were glazed, and she was panting with a sexual urge she could not quite explain to herself. But one thing she knew, Eros and Obe understood completely. She was the innocent. She was the novice in this universal game of desire. Human. Alien. It made no difference. She was under Eros' control, body and mind, right now.

Her nipples grew taut. Watching her every emotion, Eros'

eyes glowed. He moved forward. With exacting slowness, he sucked on her nipples, first one, then the other, then began to trace a line from between her breasts to her pussy with his tongue. Up and down, slowly, then back and forth, every move was calculated to arouse her, and Eros was a skilled and patient lover. Even though his eyes were half-closed, she could see that he was watching her, judging her responses to his touch.

He moved in close, flicking her clit with his tongue, and she was so swollen, so aroused, that she actually screamed with delight. Just as quickly, he moved back and smiled, his voice now husky with a desire he kept reined in. "You are close, my darling Nora. You are close. And you are going to give me and Obe quite a show."

"I don't understand," she breathed out. Show? What did he mean? She was quick to learn.

He was relentless with his mouth, his tongue, his lips, making her squeal and beg and cry with mindless abandon. He took her to the very edge, then drew back, made her body start to convulse, then stopped until she was wild for release. Nothing was important except his lovemaking. She kept getting hotter and hotter and more and more desperate for the release he held back. She flung her head back and Obe reached down and kissed her lips, her cheeks, her neck.

And then... With a gasp of raw pleasure, he took her clit into his mouth, flicking and teasing her until she moaned out loud. When he stopped and looked up at her, she was helplessly in his grip.

"Please don't stop," she begged. "Eros, please. I am going to come!"

"I don't want you to come," he cried. "I want you to explode."

His fingers pulled apart her innermost lips, and his mouth found the spot between her vagina and her anus, sucking hard until his tongue slipped between the folds and moved back and forth. The intimacy was too much for Nora. She cried out and arched her hips to his face and he grabbed her buttocks and pulled her close.

"Eros!"

He didn't answer. His hot lips and tongue were at her clit again, and this time she knew he was serious. His rhythm was demanding and searing to her body, and she couldn't have stopped moving to his pace, even if she had a gun to her head. He was going to drag her to the precipice... and push her over the top, screaming his name. The exquisite release buckled her legs wide open and his tongue left her clit and plunged deep into her body. And she screamed with a pleasure she didn't know existed.

Half-conscious, she felt Eros lift her gently and put her head on a pillow, then cover her with a blanket. The lights darkened to help her sleep. She was floating. But she did hear Obe address Eros and she always would remember his words.

"She was amazing. Nora is a creature made for sexual release. I almost lost control."

Eros was quiet for a moment, but as he closed the panel, his words floated to her. "I have lost control. My feelings for her are too powerful. I wish I could release everything I have into her sweet pussy and make her totally mine. Even my very essence."

"That is not good, Eros. You are the master."

"I know. It is a good thing the program is almost over. I have been too captured by this wild woman."

Chapter 9

How long she slept, was a mystery to Nora. Time seemed to have lost all meaning for her. She was ravaged, but it had been pure, unadulterated pleasure. When she did surface to reality, she did a slow inventory. Lips were swollen. Pussy was swollen. Breasts still throbbed with the release of orgasm. If the world ended right now, she wouldn't care. Nothing could upset her. Or so she thought.

When Eros strode into the room, looking remarkably chipper, she looked at him in surprise. He had recovered a lot faster than she had, but then again, she hadn't satisfied him. A wave of guilt washed over her, then common sense. It was his experiment, not hers. She didn't make the rules. It felt good to not feel guilty.

"What are you thinking?" Eros asked, studying her. His presence filled the room.

"Just how I am changing." Nora smiled at him.

"You certainly are," he said with a frown, and her smile turned down at the corners. "What is it? I can see that something is wrong. You sound sullen, Nora. Get up."

Something sparked in Nora. She jumped up, put on her

robe, and met his gaze with eyes flashing, her hands turning into fists. "What power you have! All you have to do is say something and it is a command."

Eros grabbed her around the waist and lifted her right off her feet. "I am powerful. But learn this, Nora! Power is a two-edged sword. It can be used for domination, like the men you have had in your life, or it can be used to protect. Don't be scornful of a powerful being. A woman giving birth is power-ful. A man defending his family is powerful. Don't you want power then?"

She just stared at him, knowing she had lost this argument.

"Answer me!" He gave her the slightest shake.

"Yes. You are right."

He plopped her back in the chair, and before she could say anything, he pointed to the CCIB. "I have something to show you, but it isn't going to make you happy. That is why I was abrupt."

Nora's chin quivered. "I'm sorry. I shouldn't have acted like that."

Eros flipped the CCIB open and pressed a few buttons. It was a dark screen. He began to pace back and forth as it searched for a signal. His presence filled the room.

"What is it, then?" she asked.

The Eluvian walked slowly back and forth, watching her reaction. "Tell me about your father."

That was a complete surprise. "My father? He was a brute."

"Tell me more. Describe him physically."

"Tall, muscular, heavy in middle age, he carried his body like a weapon. Most people were afraid of him, with good reason. He was a long-haul truck driver until an accident side-lined him for six months' recovery time, and I think he got worse. That was what my mother told me. He went back to work but only for local companies and began to drink a lot more. His mood was always testy, but alcohol made him mean. My mom sported a lot of black eyes and swollen lips from his blows."

"It must have been terrible for you." It was a statement, not a question.

Nora didn't deny it. She twisted her hands in her lap. "It was. I was scared to death of him when he started drinking. So was my mother, but she tried to hide it from me. When he went after me, she would take the blows for me. I still feel so guilty."

"Why didn't she leave him?"

"She was a foreigner in this country, with no family. She didn't have an education, or even a job. She didn't speak English well. A lot of times, he hid the car keys so she couldn't leave. Still, many nights we learned to run out the back door and hide in the shed until he finally passed out." Nora's voice choked with emotion.

"When you were under sedation, you told me he had abandoned you and your mother when you were about twelve?"

"Yes. And later, my mother thought he had died. Someone told her about an accident involving a truck pile-up in California. Several trucks went off a cliff and the drivers were never found. It was part of his old truck route. My mother was sick by then, so we never pursued it. Frankly, we were both glad he wouldn't be coming back. But it was wishful thinking. The day you found me, he had left a note on my door. That was why I was distracted and didn't notice Dale."

"Did you contact him?"

"Of course not."

Eros gave her a long, enigmatic stare. She knew him well enough by now to know that he was deciding something.

"What are you trying to tell me?" Her hands gripped the table rim.

Eros didn't mince words. "You are right. He is very much alive. And he has returned to Ridge Valley. And already, he is causing you problems. Obe has been watching him closely."

"What!" It wasn't a question so much as a scream of pain. Without realizing it, she began to shake with fear. Eros saw her reaction and reached out, taking her fingers in his giant hands.

"Nora. Nora. You have nothing to fear from him. You have me now, and my protection."

"Why now?" She looked at Eros in bewilderment.

"Evidently, Dale and Jimmy Brady, your friend's ex, have been going around town saying you girls were abducted by aliens. The story has gotten a lot of publicity, and your father heard about it and decided to get in on the action. He and his woman set up a *Go Fund Me* account called *Find Nora*. Right now, the account has brought in over three-thousand dollars."

Nora sat back, not surprised, but still disgusted. "What a bastard. My poor mother lies dead and buried with just a cross to mark her grave, and he's making money off me, probably thinking I'm dead, too."

"Why just a cross?" Eros asked.

"I haven't been able to afford a decent stone marker. I've been saving for it, but the divorce took all my savings." She looked at Eros. There was real compassion on his face now. "I'm not complaining. Just saying, she and I had a hard life, and he was the main cause."

"Yes. I can see that." He shook his head thoughtfully as he touched the screen of the CCIB. "I think there is something you must see. I would spare you the pain, but in the long run, it wouldn't help you in your development."

"How can I see him?"

"He's going to be on television in three minutes."

"You can beam into the television station?"

"Yes." He squeezed her hands at the wrists. "You are

powerful, Nora, and very brave. You can see him and not cower. And I am here for you if you need me."

Nora felt a knot start to form in the pit of her stomach. "You really think this is a good idea?"

"Yes. It is best to confront our demons." He smiled. "Trust me."

She met his gaze, and something began to melt inside her. Eros was the strongest living creature she had ever met. If Eros thought she was strong, then perhaps she was.

"Okay. Turn it on." She moved closer to the screen and settled in the safety of Eros' powerful arms. He kissed the top of her head in a silent gesture of support.

Then she saw her father's face and gasped. Recognition was like experiencing a car crash. Her heart pounded faster than any doctor would like to hear, and she felt lightheaded. Still, she managed to look calm and forced herself to focus.

The interview was being conducted at the television station. A female anchor Nora didn't recognize was sitting next to a large, burly man in a red hunting jacket. He was bald and he should have shaved three days ago.

"Is it him?" Eros asked.

"Oh, yes." Nora couldn't suppress the shiver that ran through her, but the anchor was starting to talk so she listened carefully.

"Well, folks, as you all know, the citizens of Ridge Valley, Ohio, have been the center of attention this week. Two men I interviewed yesterday have sworn that aliens abducted their girlfriends and two other women. The car the women were driving was found in a secluded area of the county called Creepy Woods, known for its scary reputation. All we know for sure is that the women, all age twenty-two, were not in the car when authorities arrived and haven't been seen since. No one knows what happened to them, but there are a lot of theories." The anchor paused

for breath, then she continued. *"But one thing is for sure; they are missing. Today, I have the father of one of the women. Elmer Dawson is leading a search for his daughter, Nora Dawson Glower."*

The camera panned to Elmer Dawson's face. He looked as mean and as rotten as she remembered him, only older.

The anchor continued. *"Mr. Dawson, you aren't from this area, I believe."*

"I was. Born and raised here on a farm nearby. Became a trucker when I married my Swedish wife, darling Berga. But when my dear wife died, I upped stakes and moved to Kansas."

"Liar! He was long gone."

"But what about your daughter, Nora? She was quite young when you left."

He looked a little baffled by the question but craftily bounced back. *"Well, she married young, to Dale Glower. Nice guy!"*

"I'm going to kill him!" Nora jumped up and actually pounded the table. Eros watched her with fascination.

The anchor looked like she was going to argue a point, probably about Nora's age, but decided against it. *"So why did you return to your hometown?"*

"I saw that my baby girl…"

"Liar!"

"…Nora was missing, so I did what any good father would do. I came to search for her." Dawson tried to look upset and managed to look like he was constipated.

Nora turned beet red. "Here we go. This is the real reason he's back."

The anchor turned to face the camera squarely. *"So, how can we help?"*

"It costs a lot to search for a missing person." Dawson let down his guard and managed to sound angry.

The anchor had to bring this to an end, so she stepped in. *"Mr. Dawson has set up a* Go Fund Me *page, called* Find Nora, *and the fund has raised almost three-thousand dollars in just three days."*

The camera panned back to Elmer, who held up Nora's high school portrait. *"Please help me find my baby girl."*

"Can you believe the nerve of that man?" Nora fought the urge to slam something.

"Yes, I can. How do you feel right now?" Eros watched her closely.

Nora got up and began to pace around the table. "How do I feel? How do I feel?"

"Yes. How do you feel?" He leaned toward her. "I want to know your raw emotions right now."

Nora stopped dead in her tracks and raised her clenched fist. "I feel rage at him. Rage at what he did to my mother and me. Rage at his false concern and lies! And rage that he is making money off me, with no real concern about my whereabouts. I could be lying in a ditch somewhere, dead, or dying."

"Very true," Eros agreed. "He is not a very developed human."

"You can say that again."

"He's not a very developed human."

Nora stared at Eros. "You just said that."

"I know, but you told me to say it again." Eros shook his head. "I see my mistake. You were just saying a phrase. We Eluvians don't have toss away phrases. But never mind. Go on."

Nora almost laughed. It took some of the steam out of her. She shook her head. "If he was here right now, I would pop him one right on the nose. As hard as I could."

"Good."

"I want to hit him as hard as I can, just like he hit us." Nora swore softly under her breath.

"And Dale. What do you want to do to him?"

"Line him up right next to my father! I want to nail them both."

"Good girl. Righteous anger is good. As long as you don't really act on it."

Nora put her hands on her hips and challenged Eros. "I don't get it. It's good to feel rage, but don't act on it?"

"Not in a negative way. You must act in a positive way."

Eros patted his lap, beckoning her to him. She didn't hesitate. Nora slid onto his lap and put her head on his shoulder. "I promised my mother I would never marry a man like my father and look what I did. I married someone even worse than my father."

"This, we have discovered, is common with humans. People go to the familiar even when it is not good for them. It takes time to evolve and understand your own flaws and fix them. Don't be too hard on yourself."

Nora digested this. Some of what Eros said was starting to be clear to her.

"But why did you marry him? I want to understand, but far more important, is that you should understand, too."

Nora looked up at him, trying to put the pieces together. For the first time, she was starting to see her world more clearly. "Dale grew up tough, in and out of foster homes and reform schools. But he started out being nice to me. I felt like he understood me, needed me. I had taken care of my mother, and after she died, I was lost. But Dale pointed out that he needed me, too, so we eloped."

"Did he?"

"Did he what?" she asked.

"Did he understand you?"

She looked at Eros and met his gaze. No matter how badly it humiliated her, she now had to really face the truth. Even to her closest friends, she had never uttered the words. "No. All he really needed was a punching bag. I am so ashamed."

"It is not your shame, but his."

"I still want to kick the hell out of them both." Without thinking, she put out her hand.

Eros took it and gently rubbed the inside of her palm. "Of course, you do. You wouldn't, but you are right."

Nora eyed him, sensing a trap. "Why wouldn't I?"

"Because you are a good human being, and violence is never the answer.'

"I'm confused."

"Violence is only justified in self-defense. If your father barged in here and tried to hit you, of course, you could hit him back. Although, I must tell you that I would reach him first. But now that you have acknowledged your anger, you must learn to let it go. It will hurt you more than him."

Nora filled her cheeks with air and blew out. It was her way of relieving frustration, and there were just too many things going on her life right now to deal with it all.

Eros gently turned her chin to face him. "I am so proud of you. You have learned a great lesson."

"I did?" Nora blinked back tears of confusion.

"Yes. When you first came to this craft, you were terrified of your father and Dale, but today, when I asked you how you felt, you only said you were full of rage. You never once mentioned that you were afraid, and I never saw it on your face. You feel safe here with me, don't you? For the first time in your life, you have been able to put aside the fear and let a normal reaction come to the surface."

"But you just said rage wasn't good."

"No. Rage and anger at an unjust situation is normal. You must learn not to cower, but to respond with a positive solution." Eros laughed. "You are a feisty woman, Nora. I am very proud to be your lover."

Nora flushed beet red. His eyes were so penetrating. He knew so much about her, more than anyone she had ever known. He was demanding a lot from her. Could she trust him? Emotionally and physically? Yesterday, she would have said no, but now, just perhaps…

He stood up and tilted her chin up to face him. With the utmost gentleness, he reached down and swept his lips across hers. For all its briefness, it was a very intimate kiss. She gasped as he drew away.

Eros reached over and pushed her hair out of her eyes. "That's better."

"What was that?" she asked.

He smiled. "A little curl. A little golden curl."

Chapter 10

Nora was just starting to get sleepy for the night. The lights were dim, and soft music was playing somewhere, although she couldn't identify the musical instrument. Her eyes were getting heavy when the far panel slipped open and Obe entered the room. He was wearing a black silky bathrobe. Nora opened her eyes wide.

"What's wrong?" she demanded, sitting up on her bed.

Obe smiled. In the dim light, his silver eyes shone like two stars.

"Why, nothing at all. Eros sent me. He is receiving communications from the mother ship and he wants to make sure this is done properly."

"*What* is done properly?"

Obe sat down on the bed carefully, aware that she was small compared to his size. He held up a vial. It was the same thing Eros had inserted into her yesterday to help soften her vagina.

Nora pushed herself upright. "Wait. I want to ask you a few questions? Is that okay?"

He grew serious. "I think so. It depends on what you want to know."

"Eros said you are an Eluvian, like him."

"Yes."

"But you are wearing a suit that makes you appear human."

"Yes."

"How does it fit? Do you take it off when you want to sleep?"

Obe burst out laughing and his eyes flashed like shooting stars.

"What?" Nora asked, a little hurt. She must sound pretty stupid, but she wanted to know.

"I love the questions humans ask. You are a race of very curious beings."

"Well? I'm waiting."

"When we star travelers are done with our training, the first level is being an Observer."

"That's what Eros said."

"Yes. Very good. You are very smart." He nodded approvingly. "We are outfitted with our human body suits and then put into them by cellular transmission. When our mission is done, the human suit will be removed."

Nora frowned.

"What?" Obe was immediately curious.

"Don't take this the wrong way, but even though you look human, you actually don't. Your skin is way too white. Even albinos, people without skin pigment, are darker than you. And your eyes, no one has silver eyes that flash like yours do."

"I don't take it the wrong way. Our scientists did this on purpose. We don't want humans to come too close unless we actually do want them to. You can't believe how people avoid me. Not rudely, but instinctively. Humans sense their own kind. Dogs and cats, however, are delighted to see us."

"One more question."

"Some of our information is astronomically sensitive."

"Astronomically sensitive?" Nora pondered the words for a moment. "As in sex."

Obe laughed. "No. As in secret space communications, locations, energy level data. You humans aren't the only secretive beings in the universe. Some life forms are good, and some are not, but usually to advance to the next level, space beings must rid themselves of the evil parts of their makeup."

"That's good, but why?"

"Because evil is toxic, and it destroys those who embrace it. Hate never solves a problem."

Nora was silent for a long time, thinking about her father and Dale. She told Obe what she and Eros had discussed, her hatred for her father and Dale. But did her hate hurt them at all? Not much, she realized.

"You are thinking of your ex-husband and your father." Obe took her hand and rubbed the inside of her palm to soothe her.

Nora's lower lip trembled. "Yes. It isn't fair. They cause so much pain and then get off scot-free, and not only are the victims hurt, then their righteous anger eats them up. Not fair!"

"Not fair, I agree." Obe tilted her face toward him. "But very little is fair in the universe. It is how you deal with your problems that advance your survival."

"You are very advanced compared to us. It is fun sitting here learning about the universe."

"Yes. Our civilization is thousands and thousands of years older than yours. You humans are just babies. But with a little luck, you will all learn."

"I hope so."

"And I sense that all these questions are to delay what I came here to do. Am I right?"

Nora blushed.

Before she could protest, Obe flipped her onto her stomach and pinned her down. "I like to administer this vial in my own way," he explained.

Nora struggled for a moment then realized it was useless.

Slowly, Obe pulled up her nightgown until her fanny was there for him to see. "Very nice." He stroked her for a moment and then began to pull her legs apart. "I enjoyed our lovemaking. I look forward to more when we are on Earth. You can summon me at any time."

"Wait. Wait!" Nora struggled, and he released her for a moment.

"What?"

"You are very nice, Obe, and I really loved it when you made love to me, but I think my heart has been taken by Eros. Don't be upset."

"I'm not upset. That is why he has chosen me to watch you and keep you safe."

"Then, why can't I go with him?"

Obe kept her fanny bare, but he tapped his fingers, thinking about her question. "It is simple. Humans are not physically developed to withstand space travel. Quite simply, you would quickly die. Perhaps someday, but not now."

Nora thought about this for a moment. "So, you can only come to us. We can't come to you."

"Yes. That is correct."

Eros had been right about Obe, too. After their passionate lovemaking, she now felt close to him. She was not ashamed of her arousal as his fingers, warm and strong, felt their way into her vagina.

"Very nice."

She heard a little click as the cap came off, and Obe inserted the vial into her vagina. To her intense surprise, he removed the vial and replaced it with his index finger, massaging and stroking her.

Nora could barely breathe, the sensations were so intense and intimate. Just when she thought she might start to come, he removed his finger and she cried out in disappointment.

He laughed. "Just preparing you for Eros, and he is the master."

Nora gasped and then gasped again, for she heard another click, and suddenly, Obe was separating her buttocks and circling her rectum with his fingers.

"No. Too intimate!" Nora screamed, but he ignored her. Before she could protest, he inserted the bottle tip into her ass and slowly, very slowly, began to fill her with the hot liquid that relaxed her muscles. His finger followed, and she cried out in surprised pleasure. He rubbed and rubbed.

"You are trembling," Obe noted. "Do you need to relieve yourself? Sometimes that happens."

"No!" Nora gasped but she prayed she wouldn't shame herself because all her nether parts felt on fire. At last, he withdrew and sat back. "What?" she asked after a few minutes when she could finally speak. She turned and looked at him. "What?"

"You are a very passionate woman, Nora. Eros is very lucky to be your master.

"I have no master, Obe. No one is my master." She spoke clearly and slowly.

Obe got up, smiling.

"What?" she demanded.

He left the room, never saying another word.

Chapter 11

Borgo woke Nora up with a bunch of slurpy kisses.

She opened her eyes to see Tria opening and closing doors, staring into space, then sighing out loud. It was clear that the Trieluvian was distracted and upset.

"Is something wrong?" Nora immediately picked up on Tria's distress. She sat up in bed and sat Borgo on the floor. The little creature immediately jumped back up on the bed.

"Not your problem," Tria mumbled dismissively.

Nora wouldn't let her get away with it. She put on her robe, stood, and moved to the table. Still standing, she confronted Tria. "But something is wrong, isn't it? Is it me? Have I done something stupid?"

"No, not you." Tria waved her hand for Nora to sit down. "Have some coffee."

"Then, who?"

Tria took a deep breath. "Your friend, Jessie."

Nora almost dropped her cup. "Is she ill?"

"No. She is fine. Actually, more than fine." Tria slumped into the other chair and gathered up Borgo.

"What is the problem?" Nora persisted. She knew she had

to go slowly with Tria, but she wanted some answers. Jessie was her closest friend.

"The problem is that Jessie had a more powerful aura than we anticipated, and it has caused problems with her master. It looks like their relationship will have to be terminated today."

Nora gulped. "When you say terminated—"

"She will be sent home. Today is the fifth day of a seven-day study, and in itself, that isn't too bad, but there are complications."

"Like?"

"Well, Eros Commander X and the other project leaders are now re-evaluating this study and the one to follow. The next study was supposed to start in 2100 c.e. your time. But it might be pushed up."

"What is it?"

"I can't tell you."

"Well, then, tell me why you are so upset."

"I don't want to get stuck on that project. Another five-hundred years circling Earth is going to drive me nuts. I want to expand my horizons." Tria tilted her purple head to the left and then to the right as one of her antennae drooped in despair.

Nora didn't know what to say. "Will this affect me in any way?"

"Not that I know of, but everything has gone so off kilter because of you and your friends that who can tell!"

"Have Gilly and Rose been causing problems, too?" Nora couldn't help asking.

Tria gave her a baleful look. Her red eye expanded, then narrowed, and Nora understood.

"But I've been good. No trouble with me? Right?"

Tria stood up. "That remains to be seen. I have a hunch that you might be the most dangerous one of all."

Nora sat musing over Tria's words for a long time after the Trieluvian took Borgo and left. What in heaven's name was happening? Gilly was the wild one of their quartet. Gilly was the ringleader, the fighter, the fearless one. Rose was the innocent, raised by her maiden aunt. Jessie was the thoughtful one of the group. She would never cause trouble. Would she? Life had changed so much for Nora. Had it been the same for Jessie, Gilly, and Rose?

As she thought about all the different possibilities that might play out, another thought came to her. Tria said today was day five of the study. She still had to have intercourse with Eros, and no time had been discussed. And even far more important to her, was the realization she didn't want to leave him. She was happy here. She was in love with Eros, and she was pretty sure he thought she was special, too. What would life be without him? She couldn't imagine. But Obe had been clear. She couldn't follow Eros into space. It would be a death sentence.

To distract herself from such depressing thoughts, she began to study the CCIB. Eros had said she could turn it on if she pressed the white button. It was set to locate her father. Did she dare? Did she have the nerve to watch him without Eros' bracing presence.

She took a deep breath. She did! Damn it, she did! She reached out and pressed the white button.

At first, it was a blur. White lines kept swirling around the globe, but as she sat still and waited, the lines slowed down, coalesced, merged, and formed into figures. Suddenly, it was as clear as a television screen.

There was her father, sitting down on the grass. She could tell he was outside because of the trees in the background.

They looked familiar, but he was talking to someone and she needed to hear. She leaned in closer.

"That girl has been a problem since the day she was born. I didn't want no kids, but that fat sow I married got herself pregnant, and then who had to pay the bills?"

Sow! Her beautiful, gentle mother! Nora felt anger surge within her, but she forced it down. What her father was saying was too important to miss.

"If I had been around, I would have warned you off her, boy!" Her father took out a pint bottle from his pocket and took a long swig.

His companion chortled agreement, and it wasn't a pleasant sound.

Who is he talking to? Nora wondered.

She heard a rustle behind her and Tria leaned over her shoulder. "You can turn up the audio by pressing this dot, and you can expand your view by moving this line back and forth. To the left, will let you see more."

Nora did as she was told and immediately cursed. Dale Gower was cross-legged on the ground next to her father. He looked loopy, too. Probably drunk, himself. He seemed to look around.

"Why are you staying out here? This place gives me the creeps."

"Safer that way."

"Safer?"

"Yeah. Years back, I had to leave town in a hurry if you get my drift. Some young buck didn't like what I did to his ma. Said I raped her and then beat her up. That son now carries a three-inch scar on his cheek for taking me on. But ten years have passed. He's grown even bigger now, and meaner, and I been told he's looking for me."

"That wouldn't be Harry McKow by any chance?"

"And that would be a yes!" Her father laughed, not the least repentant.

Dale actually looked over his shoulder nervously. *"You don't want to be messing with the McKow clan. They're the toughest bunch in the county, and they* are *looking for you. And they mean business."*

Nora's father laughed. It was a nasty screech, and he showed Dale his hunting knife. *"I'm ready."*

"That ain't going to be any good against bullets." Dale actually said something that made sense.

"Forget it." Her father was nodding up and down, in agreement with himself for something he hadn't uttered out loud.

"Yes. Like I said, that girl might actually be a good turn for me after all. The Go Fund Me *page is making a lot of cash. How is the one you and Jimmy Brady put up?"* He wiped the back of his mouth with his hand and gave Dale a sly look. *"No danger those girls are going to show up, is there?"*

"Naw. The aliens got them!"

Her father cursed and threw the empty liquor bottle at Dale.

"Why did you do that?" yelled Dale, standing up.

"Shut up about that crap of aliens. You don't think I believe it for a minute, do you? You and Brady scared those girls right out of the county, or did you kill them and bury them somewhere?"

Dale brushed himself off. *"Wished we had, but I'm not lying when I say this. Whoever took 'em wasn't human."*

He strode off, wobbling around objects in his path.

Nora moved the lever back to her father. He was settling in for a nap. His knapsack was his pillow. *Where is he?* she wondered. And then he shifted, and true horror, followed by rage, overcame her. There was the cross marking her mother's grave.

The bastard was camping out at the cemetery. The nerve of him made her sick.

Tria left her alone after she turned off the CCIB. The alien sensed that Nora needed to be alone to work things out in her head.

No one had ever successfully stopped Elmer Dawson when he was bad. Her mother had tried and been beaten for her trouble. The McKow woman was sexually assaulted, beaten, and had evidently failed, along with her son. Nora had failed. She had been too young to confront him and had run at the first sound of rage.

How many other people had he harmed?

Chapter 12

"**D**o you want to talk?" Eros had entered the room and scooped her up in his arms.

"Not really. I'm still thinking through everything. Did Tria fill you in?" She tilted her head and looked up at him.

"Yes, she did. Dale and your father have become friends. Or as much friends as they are capable of being."

"Looks like it." Nora didn't want to go there right now. Instead, she changed the subject. "What is going on with Jessie?"

"Tria told you that, too? She's a little talker today, isn't she?" To Nora's surprise, he stood up and carried her toward the shower.

Nora had to admit that she was eager. "Yes. No. A little."

He laughed. "I think I will show you the problem, better than tell you."

"Show me?" She eyed him with a little grin. "Is that in the protocol."

He didn't answer the question. "First, a quick shower."

They both stripped naked with ease, and instantly, Nora

was enveloped with the scented, warm suds. Eros massaged the soap all over her body and then she worked on him. When she reached his penis, he covered her hand and stopped her.

"Why?" she asked.

"You'll see."

He carefully wrapped her in a silky red robe and wrapped a white towel around his waist. Then he reached up and pulled a silver lever.

Nora heard another panel slide open and realized they were going into a part of the craft she hadn't seen before. To her surprise, Eros took her hand and led her out of one of the sliding panels. They entered a compartment that was filled with light. It reminded Nora of an elevator, but there were no buttons. Eros just said a command she couldn't understand, and in moments, the panel slid open.

"After you, darling. Welcome to the universe." Eros stepped aside to let her go first.

Nora stepped out and gasped. They were in a compartment made of glass, or whatever clear substance Eluvians had invented. She felt as if they were floating in space. The moon was a large yellow orb that lit up the sky. Stars hovered around them. The earth was somewhere far below.

"I feel like we are outside," she whispered.

"We are in a viewing room. We can activate this room if we want to get a good idea of what is happening in space. See! Over there is an asteroid coming our way."

Eros pointed to a speck in the distance. Nora whirled around and watched the speeding rock come toward them, growing from a speck of dirt to the size of a car in under a minute. It gave off faint sparks of light as it raced across space.

Will it hit us?" she asked breathlessly.

Eros laughed. "No. Those lights you are seeing are Phosinian navigators. They will guide the asteroid away from us."

"Marvelous. I feel like I'm floating in space. It's like being inside a glass ball," she cried out, delighted with the view. It was a fabulous feeling.

She put the palm of her hand against the glass in awe and watched thousands of stars in the surrounding sky. Eros came up behind her and put a protective arm around her waist.

"There's Earth, and behind it, the setting sun." He pointed to the left. "The moon is rising now."

A lovely, warm, pink light outside encircled the craft. The light came from creamy lights outside the window. All her senses were heightened. The shower had caressed her skin and made her feel sensual and wild. Her ears picked up the sound of music, a throbbing beat that matched the beat of her heart. It pulsed and demanded action.

Eros likes music. Her eyes opened wide when he kissed a drop of water off her nose.

"A nice tune." Nora smiled haltingly. "Dawn is the name of that song. I love that time of the day. Especially in summer."

"I know. I saw it in your memory folder."

"My memory folder?" Nora was nonplussed, especially since Eros came and sat on the bed.

He put one powerful arm around her and pulled her close. "Yes. All your memories are neatly organized in a folder for review if we want to do so."

"And did you?" Nora's voice was sharp with a sense of violation. She pulled away and he released her. She wanted to slap the little half-smile that hovered on his lips—his beautiful, full lips.

"Only the pleasant ones. That is how I came to know you liked this time of day."

"You do understand that what you did was a direct violation of my privacy."

"Yes. But necessary." He ran his hand through her hair.

"Nice. And I like the way your eyes shine when you are angry. We will make love soon, and it will be nice."

Suddenly shy, Nora moved away and faced the glass. Light was flashing across the sky.

"Moonbeams," Eros whispered as he edged away and sat down in a large chair in the center of the room. "Actually, they are sunbeams, but the sunlight is reflecting off the moon, creating that effect."

He was so intelligent, and he knew so much more than she would ever know. She looked out into space. It was Eros' world, and he soon would be returning to its vastness.

Her heart fluttered with sadness. "I will miss you."

"I know. And I will miss you, too. You have become very special to me."

Nora turned and smiled at him. Her hair was starting to turn silver gold in the moonlight and fell to her shoulders in long wavy, loose curls. "You look like the captain of the universe in that chair."

"Well, I *am* a captain of the universe." He smiled and placed a red velvet pillow at his feet. "I come here alone, to think things through."

"Powerful and fearless," Nora teased as she drifted over to his side and sat down on the pillow. "The master of all he sees."

"Am I your master, Nora?"

She looked down. She knew she loved him, but she couldn't bring herself to call him master. Something deep inside her wanted to acknowledge him as master, but the bruised and broken part of her soul was too afraid.

He seemed to sense her confusion and didn't press her. Instead, he ran his large hand through her damp hair and lightly massaged her scalp. "Very pretty."

She curled up between his naked legs and rested her head on his left thigh. It was impossible not to realize that her face was just inches away from his enormous cock. The urge to slip her hand under the towel made her bite her lip in surprise.

For once, he misread her thoughts. "Are you still worried about your friend Jessie?"

Nora took a deep breath and went for it. "Yes. I don't understand what happened. Tria was very cryptic."

"Tria is often cryptic, but she is well-trained in keeping things secret. Actually, I'm surprised she let her guard down enough to let you know there was a problem at all." He sighed. "Like me, she has become very fond of you."

Nora's eyes opened in surprise. "So, can you tell me what happened?"

"I think I can show you." He laughed at her surprised face. "But let me start at the beginning."

"Okay."

"Each master is given a lot of leeway in how they proceed with the experiments. Jessie's master, whom she called The Voice, preferred to conduct his studies under the cloak of invisibility."

"Can you do that?" Nora asked, interrupting him.

"Of course. I guess I never told you that as advanced beings, we have mastered construction and deconstruction finite order—"

"What?"

"Invisibility. But it takes a lot of energy and can only be used for a short period of time, a few hours at most, and a lot of concentration is required."

"I'm glad you chose to be visible."

"I thought you would. But Jessie did quite well."

"What was the problem with Jessie?"

"It was The Voice who had the problem."

"And that was?" Nora urged him on.

"His feelings for Jessie were so great that when she performed oral sex on him—"

"How could she do that if she couldn't—"

Eros sighed. "Just stay with me, Nora. Okay?"

Nora tentatively put one of her little hands on his powerful thigh. "Sorry."

"It's okay." When she went to remove her hand, he grasped it and held it to his skin. "I like that. Your touch is soft, but compelling. Perhaps you could go a little farther up.'

Nora took a deep breath and began to edge higher and higher, and before long, she was on the edge of the towel.

"Put your hand underneath."

"Tell me what happened." She laughed, slipping her hand under the towel and moving upward toward his upper thigh.

"She performed so well that when he reached climax…" Eros stopped. Nora's fingers were teasing his balls and he closed his eyes in pleasure.

"Go on."

"He climaxed so hard that his semen broke the shield of invisibility and was all over her."

Nora stopped and stared at him. "That was bad?"

"It wasn't good. It meant his feelings for her were greater than his control. It has never happened before. The commanders in the mother ship are in an uproar." He shifted slightly. "You see, you human women are something special."

Nora looked up at his face. His eyes were still closed, and he was flushed. Something bloomed inside her, a flower of desire that she couldn't control. Did she have that power? Could she make Eros lose control?

With infinite slowness, she caressed his balls and noticed that the towel was rising. She turned to position herself on her knees and carefully removed the towel, revealing Eros in all his glory. He was huge.

Her little hands circled his cock and began to move up and down. "Do you like that?" she purred.

"By all the stars in the universe, I love your little hands moving up and down, slowly, then faster."

Nora laughed, loving her power, loving his power. On her knees, she edged forward, pushing her full breasts against his balls, and he groaned and pleaded for mercy.

She rose up slightly and began to lick his cock, and he moaned. With her hands and her tongue, she worked him into a frenzy. His powerful hands clutched the arms of the chair, his fingers red with the pressure.

"Use your teeth, you minx!" he cried out.

She ribbed his giant cock with her teeth, licking and biting in a way that teased him to beg for more. He was powerful, but so was she. Even on her knees in front of him, she was the pleasure giver, the lover he demanded her to be. And it was wonderful. She loved it when he trembled under her touch and moaned when she licked higher and higher.

As she felt him getting closer and closer to the edge, she cupped his cock with her mouth, and he screamed for mercy. Her hands flew lightly, her fingers pushed up and down, until he arched his back and screamed out her name, "Nora! Nora! Nora!"

His semen spilled into her hands and across her breasts and she collapsed against his cock and abdomen, breathing hard.

They lay that way for a long time. The light faded into a dark blue sky peppered with stars. Eros entwined his fingers in her silky hair, humming a little tune.

The moonbeams grew brighter, more intense, when she finally raised her head and smiled. "I think I understand what happened with Jessie and The Voice."

"Believe me, I really understand. Poor bastard. He didn't stand a chance!"

Chapter 13

The next day, Tria was even more subdued when she brought Nora's breakfast. Even Borgo wasn't himself. All of his ears drooped at odd angles. Nora thought he resembled a ball of tangled white yarn.

Still dreamy from the day before, Nora munched on a piece of toast. She knew she should choose her words carefully. "I saw the glass room yesterday," she volunteered.

"I know." Tria was totally disinterested.

Of course, she knew. Everything that happened between her and Eros was probably recorded in the case study listed as Nora Dawson. The whole, beautiful experience, so magical to Nora, was commonplace for Tria.

"It was beautiful to see the stars and the moonbeam."

"It's nice," Tria agreed, but it was an absentminded reply. It was clear her mind was elsewhere. Borgo jumped onto Nora's lap and she played with the animal, allowing Tria time to snap out of her mood. But Tria remained silent.

Nora took a breath and ventured a guess. "Still problems on this project?"

"You ought to know," Tria muttered.

"Me?" Nora was really shocked. She didn't have to face her confusion. "What are you talking about?"

"Nothing. I shouldn't have said that. Nothing that is happening is really your fault. It was bound to happen one day."

Nora put Borgo on the floor and stood up. She faced the Trieluvian squarely and looked up. Tria was at least one foot taller than she was. The alien's yellow eyes shifted to the ceiling.

Nora was direct. She liked Tria, but she was going to get some answers now! "What was bound to happen?"

"Jessie and the Voice have turned the entire project into a spin. The higher ups on the mother ship have decided the project is complete and we are done and leaving in a few days. Maybe less. Only the Observers will stay behind on Earth. That is why we haven't already left. There are over one-thousand of them to be replaced all over the world." Tria lifted her spindly hands and shrugged. "Obe will stay with you and your friends, but he will have a large territory to cover. They are giving him an assistant to train."

But Nora wanted to know more. "What was bound to happen? I understand Jessie and the Voice, but your behavior suggests that I have given you trouble."

Tria's red eye focused on Nora's face. "Of course, you have. You and Eros—"

"What about us?"

"Don't you realize what has happened?"

Nora shook her head. "Stop beating around the bush, Tria. Spill the beans."

Tria looked at her with true bewilderment, then looked around the room.

"What bush? What beans?"

Nora sighed. The Eluvians and Trieluvians were so literal. They didn't use expressions like humans do.

"Forget it. They are just phrases. I want you to tell me what you mean about Eros and me."

Tria nodded. "Don't you understand that he is a scientist? You are just a test subject.

Nora gulped. "I know what you mean, but for me, Eros has become far more. I love him. If I could, I would go with him."

"I know," Tria said sadly. "And your grief is half the problem."

"Half the problem?"

Tria shook her head.

"Don't you realize that he loves you, too? The master is besotted with you."

———

A long time passed after Tria left the room. Nora was torn apart by conflicting emotions; joy that Eros loved her, and sorrow that they would soon part. He could not stay in her world, and she could never follow him to his. Star-crossed lovers, that was what they were. Before she could really get depressed, Tria slipped back in the room. The alien walked over to the CCIC and pressed a button.

"I received notification from the mother ship that you might want to see this." Tria fiddled with the dials. "I think this might be important knowledge for you when you return to Earth. It concerns your father."

"Are you trying to ruin my day?" Nora joked.

Tria stared at her. "An Earth day cannot be ruined unless the Earth's rotation is thrown off course by the collision of an asteroid or a comet. But I believe you are joking."

"Yes, I was," Nora admitted.

Tria grunted a sound that could have been disapproval or Trieluvian humor. Nora was not sure which.

Tria tapped the table with one of her skinny, purple fingers. "Face facts. You will be returning to Earth soon and you will have to deal with him. I think you should keep abreast of things."

Tria was right. Nora leaned in to see what was happening.

First, there was static.

"There is a cloud of space dust coming through. It will be gone in a minute," Tria informed her.

She was right. Less than a minute later, the screen cleared of static and Nora was looking directly into the ugly face of the man who had given her life.

Elmer Dawson was sitting on the ground in the cemetery, talking on his cell phone. After a few minutes, Nora realized he was talking to his girl-friend, someone named Thelma. She wanted to turn to hang up but a look from Tria made her stay on.

Elmer was already half-plastered, and his voice was an annoying whine. "I'm telling you, sweet cheeks, I miss you. I'm stuck out in the graveyard looking at the cross of my first Mrs., with nothing but a six pack or two to keep me company."

Then he was silent. Evidently, Thelma was talking.

"I gotta keep out of sight. That Harry McKow swore he was going to beat me dead. And he's a brute. I know, I know. I shouldna done it, but you know how frisky I can get. She deserved it. Teasing me. Just like this old first wife, always lecturing me. Every blow she got was well-deserved."

Nora's hands turned into fists. If she could just reach him now, she would let him have it.

"So how much are we making on the Go Fund Me?" Elmer Dawson spit on his first wife's grave. "Three-thousand-five-hundred-thirty-four dollars! That's wonderful. We gonna go to the casino in West Virginia, baby! You keep up the good work!"

He hung up and took a swig of beer. "Three-thousand-five-hundred-

thirty-four dollars! My Thelma is a smart one!" He threw the empty bottle at the cross marking his late wife's grave. "Not like you!"

It was then, Nora could see the grave clearly. It was covered with empty beer bottles. It was so disrespectful, she wanted to weep. With a heavy heart, she turned off the CCIB. If Harry McKow was looking for revenge, then Elmer Dawson deserved anything sent his way.

Eros found her still sitting at the table, brooding about what she had heard.

He sat down, giving her space, and letting her tell her story in her own good time.

"Thank you," she said to him, her face serious.

"For what?"

"For giving me the time to think things out about my father… and Dale."

"Not a problem. Many problems have to be worked out in silence." He reached out and touched the CCIB. "I gather you saw something unpleasant."

Nora filled him in, not sparing any details.

"What are you going to do? Do you have a plan?"

"Yes." Nora nodded emphatically. "I know you are all into forgiveness, forget and forgive, but I can't. If you could have seen him tossing beer bottles on my mother's grave…"

Her voice broke and Eros reached out and took her hand, kissing the inside of her wrist.

"I might have confused you. Let me explain. It is good to acknowledge your emotions, even anger. Especially anger. But then you must deal with that anger correctly. Dale and your father are two perfect examples of people who have let the anger within them consume their lives. And you know the result."

"Do I ever!"

"I don't want that for you, my love."

My love. Her heart sang. *My love.* It made Nora's heart skip a beat to hear him say that to her. "I see what you are saying, but how do I deal with it?"

"With your father, I think you should confront him."

Nora stared at Eros with shock. "When I return to Earth?"

He laughed. "Yes. But safely. Bring the police with you. Or Obe."

"I'm leaving now?"

"Yes. The study has been cut short. The entire Eluvian fleet is leaving tomorrow. Everything has been set up for you. Obe is a master of disguises." Eros tilted his head and looked at her. "Why are you crying?"

"Because I will miss you terribly."

"And I you. But there is something else we must discuss, another change of plans."

Nora thought Eros looked hopeful, but she couldn't ask because a buzzer had gone off. Eros stood up suddenly and read a message on his watch. "You have to leave now! There is an asteroid approaching that will cause ripples in the gravitational field."

"Why can't I just come with you?" Nora protested. "I don't care if I die."

"Well, I do! You would never survive the trip. Just the thrust necessary for our crafts to leave your solar system, would kill you." He grabbed her arm and hauled her out of her chair. "Trust me, Nora. I know what I am doing!"

"But what about the last experiment?" Nora was shocked at her disappointment and that she had the nerve to ask. Boy, she *had* changed. "Have you forgotten?"

A sexy smile crossed Eros' lips and his blue eyes flashed sparks that looked like diamonds. "Do you really think I have forgotten?"

"No." Nora was frantic at the thought of leaving him. "I just don't understand—"

"But I do! My dear little Nora." He cupped her head in his large palm. "I will come to you tomorrow night at your home. We have a lot to discuss and there is no time now."

"But—"

"Trust me. I am completely in control."

Nora nodded. He was right. He knew so much more than she did.

Things happened quickly then. Tria came into the room with her clothes, cleaned and repaired. "Put them on. Quickly. We have no time to spare. This isn't in the prescribed experimental parameters."

"I will never see you again," Nora cried.

"Never say never. You humans are so sentimental." But Tria had tears in her yellow eyes, too, which surprised Nora.

Before she could say anything, Eros grabbed her by the arm and pulled her along, followed by Tria and Borgo. She followed him out of the familiar room and into a long hall that led to another sliding panel. It opened, revealing the world from almost ten miles above the Earth. Stars shone and the sun was a dim disc in the horizon. The moon was starting to rise.

"Jump out."

"What?" Nora turned and stared at him. "Are you crazy?"

"Jump!"

"No!"

"Wait!" The command came from Tria. She stepped forward and grabbed Nora around the waist in a hug. "We forgot to take off the diode on her scalp. Pull it off. Also, take this pill. Swallow it quickly!"

Nora did as she was told.

Eros grinned and looked at Tria. "Are the coordinates set?"

"Perfectly, Master."

Nora felt a sharp tug on her scalp. "That hurt!" she cried out.

Tria, with one perfect swing, flipped Nora out of the spacecraft and into the vastness of space. Immediately, Nora was engulfed in a beam of light and everything else disappeared.

Chapter 14

When Nora awoke, it was to the sounds of a bustling hospital. People were calling out questions, aides were delivering breakfast. A heart monitor was beeping in rhythm with her heart. She opened one eye and saw that she was attached to a lot of monitors.

She tried to think. To remember. Had the spacecraft and Eros and Tria all been a dream? No. She was sure they had been real. She opened her eyes wide and saw, to her surprise, that Gilly and Rose were in nearby beds and both were smiling at her.

"Hey, Rose, sleepyhead finally woke," Gilly teased.

Nora sat up and stared at her friends. They were already awake and waiting for her.

"It was real? I didn't imagine it?"

Gilly smiled a 'yes' and Rose beamed at her.

Nora fell back against the hospital pillows, thinking hard.

Gilly broke into her thoughts. "Someone named Obe is going to be taking care of us."

Nora went bolt upright again filled with questions.

"I know him. He's great. We're in good hands. Fill me in on what's happening. How long have we been here?"

"We all came in separately," Gilly explained. She pointed to Rose. "Rosie arrived first."

Nora took a good look at the next bed. The woman in the bed looked like Rose but seemed somehow different. It was as if Rose had been a girl but was now a woman.

"I arrived an hour later." Gilly smiled shyly. Gilly, shy? "Didn't want to say good-bye. They had to toss me out of the spacecraft."

It all came back to Nora in a rush.

"Me, too. I was pushed into a beam of light." Nora looked around. "Where's Jessie?"

"The nurse said that Jessie was dropped off in Ridge Valley by the side of the road. She's in the hospital over there."

"It was decided that since I work in the Ridge Valley emergency room, it would be better for us to be dropped off here." Rose looked a little smug. "Actually, I was the one who thought of that. My master was quite impressed."

"We just staggered into the emergency room, giving lame excuses."

Rose nodded. "Do you remember taking a pill before we left the crafts?"

Nora thought back to Tria yelling, "Stop! We forgot to remove the diode and give her a pill."

"Yes. What was it?"

"It was a disorientation pill. It was to make us look like convincing car accident victims. We stumbled and fell, and old bruises appeared on our bodies. Nothing serious. Just camouflage to make our stories sound convincing."

"And our story is?"

Rose took over. "Car accident. Jessie wandered off to get help. Ambulance came and got us. We can't remember where we were taken because of amnesia, and we have no memory of how we got to the hospital near Columbus. For some reason, they are buying it, but the press is going crazy. That's why we're holed up in this room."

Nora shook her head. "You both seem different somehow."

"You are a fine one to talk! Have you taken a good look at yourself?" Rose giggled. "You look so different. A week ago, you were deathly pale, and your hair was silver-blonde and straight. Remember me telling you to go get a blood test. I was sure you were seriously anemic."

"They told me... on the craft... that I had a bleeding ulcer."

"I knew it!" Rose, the nurse, was elated that she had been right.

Gilly jumped in with questions. "Now you look so healthy and rosy. And your hair is a mass of golden curls. What happened, girl?"

Nora grabbed a mirror in the hospital basket that contained a toothbrush and paste and took a look. "Wow. This is how I was always supposed to look. But stress and fear sapped the good health out of me."

Suddenly, a nurse entered, followed by a visitor. He was a tall man, very pale-skinned, dressed in jeans, cowboy boots, and a Cleveland Indians t-shirt. A black baseball cap covered his hair and his eyes were hidden by sunglasses.

"Look who's here, Nora. Your step-brother came all the way from Cleveland to see you."

Nora immediately recognized Obe, but with a glance, he indicated that he didn't want too much said.

"Hi, sister," he said, pulling up a chair. "How are you feeling?"

They spoke back and forth as the nurse bustled around. When she finally left the room, Nora. squealed with delight. "Have you met Gilly and Rose?"

Obe smiled in their direction. "Only in the biblical sense. Right, ladies?"

They stifled their laughter because the nurse reappeared and began to remove some of the monitors from Nora's arms.

"When can we go home?" Rose asked. "My aunt will be frantic."

"I think tomorrow. We can't rush it. We've called your aunt and explained about the car accident and the confusion with the ambulance and how you are all suffering from amnesia." The nurse paused. "The doctors are thinking that your symptoms are all a little strange. Still, we can't keep you after tomorrow."

"How are you feeling, Nora?" the nurse asked.

But Nora was saved from answering by another attendant who bustled in. "I'm here for Nora Dawson. Ready to go to X-ray?"

"Why?" Nora asked.

"Just preventative. We want to rule out all injuries before we send you home. Let's transfer her to the gurney."

"Bye." Nora waved to her friends and to Obe.

"Be watchful. The press has surrounded the hospital," he cautioned.

The attendant buckled her on the gurney with restraints.

"Hey, why those?" Nora asked.

"So you don't fall off the gurney and sue the hospital." The attendant laughed. He wheeled her out of the cubicle and down a long hall. He was young and chatty, "Boy, lady, did anyone ever tell you what gorgeous hair you have?"

"Me?"

"Yeah, sure. I never seen anyone with golden curls like you have. You're a looker."

"Thank you."

"They are running a little behind schedule. I'm leaving you

outside this door. They'll take you in about five minutes. Don't go anywhere," he joked.

"I won't," Nora promised.

Five minutes turned to ten, and Nora began to feel drowsy. She fell asleep and awoke when someone placed a heavy towel over her face. Since she was still restrained, all she could do was protest with a muffled grunt. She felt the gurney move quickly down the hall, but she wasn't really alarmed until she heard a door open and then felt the warmth of the sun on her body. Why was she outside? Now she tried to scream, but her voice was muffled by the heavy towel.

"Shut up! I won't hurt you unless you cause me trouble!"

Fear gripped her. *Who is taking me away from the hospital?* she wondered. Not Eros, Obe, or Tria. Not her father or Dale. Someone from the press? Obe had said they were outside waiting for photos. The story of the girls returning had broken on last night's evening news. Still, that was doubtful. She had never heard of a reporter kidnapping a person to get a story.

She felt herself wheeled quickly along a bumpy sidewalk, hands tied up with cord, unstrapped from the gurney and tossed unceremoniously into the back of a van. Her kidnapper yanked off the towel.

Nora looked into the face of a man she had never seen before. He was tall and thin, with high cheekbones and a rough face, made wilder by a three-day growth of beard. Even though it was hot, he was dressed in a hunting jacket and torn jeans and boots.

"What do you want with me?" She tried to remain calm. Eros had told her she was brave. Now it was time to put his faith to the test.

"Are you an alien?" Nora managed to ask as he began to close the door.

He looked at her with both shock and contempt. "Do I

look like an alien? I was born in this country, and I will die in this country when the good Lord calls me home."

"No. You misunderstood me. I mean a space alien."

He mumbled something under his breath that she didn't understand. Only the words "stupid" and "hunting dog" were clear.

Nora sighed with dark humor. Most people never experienced a kidnapping in life, but here she was, abducted for the second time in less than a full week. She wondered how long it would take Obe to discover what had happened.

Chapter 15

Her abductor secured the van door and Nora heard the lock click shut. The back of the van was locked, the windows, too, and she was separated from the cab by a thick metal screen used by dog breeders and hunters who wanted to transport their animals. The man went around to the driver's side and got in, started the engine, and carefully drove out of the lot.

Nora could see out the window, and they were soon heading out of town and down a highway. After a half hour, her abductor took a northbound exit and the van changed lanes. Then he took a right, onto a country road. Nora instantly recognized the switch. They were on a back road heading for her hometown.

She couldn't keep silent any longer. "Who are you? And what do you want with me?"

He waited for a moment then answered. His voice was gruff. "Name is Harry McKow. And I'm using you for bait to nail your father."

"How are you going to do that?"

"Well, he's holed up at the cemetery by your mother's

grave. Dale Glower been bringing him supplies. The way I planned it is I threaten to kill you, and your dad will come with me peaceful like. He and I have some serious business to settle."

"Mister McKow, I have no love for my father and he has no love for me. I don't think your plan is going to work."

"Gotta work. You're his child. No man would let his child die if he could save her." Harry was stubborn and evidently not too bright, but clearly, he was a good and determined man.

Nora wished him well and leaned back against the seat and sighed. She was pretty sure Harry McKow had made a bad calculation.

They reached the cemetery fifteen minutes later. Nora pressed her face to the window and saw her father sitting in a heap of empty bottles and camping equipment. Her mother's grave, usually so nice and neat, was a mess. The red geraniums she had planted were sticking up by their roots. When Elmer heard the van, he reached for his gun and leaped up into the air.

"Stop, or I'll shoot," he cried out.

Harry McKow ignored him. He got out of the van on the other side from Elmer, opened the door, and pulled out Nora, dragging her by the arm to the front of the van. She was barefoot and only clad in the hospital gown that tied in the back, but Harry McKow didn't seem to notice. He pulled her around the van so Elmer could clearly see her.

"Got a present for you, Elmer. Something to trade."

"Who is it? I don't want no woman."

For one moment, McKow seemed unsteady. Didn't Elmer see who he had in his grasp? "It's your daughter, you bastard low life."

Elmer took a step forward. "Nora? That ain't Nora. Nora had white-blonde, straight hair, like her ma. That girl has a head of golden curls. Also, she's way too old. Nora's a little girl."

That was it for Nora. She couldn't be silent. "I was a little girl when you abandoned me and my mother. But now I'm a woman."

Elmer tilted his head to the side. When the old lady had been truly angry at him, she had sounded like this woman. "Nora? Really? It's you?"

Harry lifted his shotgun. "Enough talk! This woman is Nora, and I'm going to kill her if you don't come along with me."

Elmer burst into laughter. "Shit. Is that your plan, McKow?"

"It is, so you come nice and kneel down, so I can tie you up, and we'll go and settle business. You hurt my mother bad and you have to pay for your crimes. As soon as you are tied up, I'll let the girl go free." He tugged on Nora's rope and she swayed sideways. "Come on. Don't dilly dally. Do what a dad has to do to save his only child."

Even with all her disappointments in her father, Nora was as surprised as Harry McKow when Elmer burst out laughing. "Go right ahead. Kill her. I don't care. I got my own life with Thelma and now a little cash. Go ahead."

"He means it, Mr. McKow. He has no love for me." Nora spoke sadly and felt McKow waver.

What was he going to do? It was clear that Harry McKow didn't have a back-up plan.

She never found out because someone came up behind him and smashed a rock into his skull. He crumpled to the ground, dropping his gun and Nora, who fell down at his feet.

Dear God, this was going from bad to worse.

Nora looked up from the muddy ground and felt sick. It was Dale who had leveled Harry McKow. He kicked the older man out of the way and picked up Nora by the hair.

"What the hell, Nora, did you dye your hair and get a perm? It looks awful nice. Too bad I'm going to beat the hell out of you." He dragged her over to Elmer and dropped her at her father's feet. "Here's your little girl and my wife."

"Ex-wife, you bastard," Nora spat out, too angry to care if he hurt her. Which, of course, he did, kicking her neatly in the ribs. Dale could be accurate when he was sober, which he seemed to be.

"Easy, easy, boy," Elmer remonstrated, but not out of love. "Don't damage the merchandise."

"I don't give a—" Dale spat out.

"Sit down, have a beer, let's think this through." Elmer opened another bottle and sat down. Close up, Nora could see that both men were less sober than she had originally thought.

Dale took a beer but didn't sit down. "Her coming back has really complicated things. Jimmy Brady and I had fun, too, just like you and Thelma, and he said no one has put in a cent since last night when these bitches all showed back up."

Elmer shook his head, burped, and took another drink. "I know. Thelma said the same thing. How much you guys have in yours?"

"Jimmy says about one-thousand-five-hundred." He nudged Nora with the toe of his boot. It hurt and when she cried out, he laughed. "How about you and Thelma?"

"A lot more than that." He thought for a moment. "I think she said almost four thousand. You know people pay more to a grieving parent than an ex-husband and boyfriend."

That got Dale thinking. Nora knew the signs because he began to pace, as if action would stimulate those brain cells. He stopped and turned on a dime. "How's about we put it all together and divide it in half. You and Thelma, half, and Jimmy and me, half?"

Elmer actually had to think about it, before realizing he

would be more than a thousand short if they did this. "No way!"

"It's only fair. You got more than we did." Dale kicked Nora again and she tried to move. He stopped her by putting his booted foot on her leg. Then he seemed to think of something. He lifted his foot and walked over to Harry McKow, who was either dead or out cold, and picked up his shotgun. "You owe me, Elmer. I saved your life. Harry McKow was gonna kill you with this gun."

Elmer guffawed. "Well, he didn't, and I don't owe you nothing. Thelma would kill me if I did."

Dale was silent. Nora knew this was a bad sign. Dale thinking was worse than Dale not thinking. She was right. Dale lifted the shotgun and pointed it straight at Elmer. Nora rolled away, hopefully out of danger.

"And if you don't, I'll kill you." Nora realized Dale meant it. "And after I kill you, I'm going to take care of Nora. And I'm going to blame it all on Harry McKow. Saw the whole thing, I'll tell the cops."

Dale came closer and pumped the shell into the chamber. "Your choice, old man."

Elmer didn't believe him. "You wouldn't dare!"

Boom!

Elmer took the shot to the stomach and keeled over.

"You should have told him, Nora. I always get what I want," Dale hissed.

Nora looked up from the ground, shaking and sick. She might not like her father, but she never wanted to see him murdered. Her eyes moved past her father slumped across her mother's grave to Harry McKow. If he wasn't dead now, he soon would be. She sat up and faced Dale. "Am I next?"

Oddly, she felt strangely calm. Death didn't frighten her anymore, along with the fear of pain. The only great regret she had was that she wouldn't see Eros again.

It was her calmness that unsettled Dale. He wanted her to cringe, to plead. But there she was, sitting in the mud, wearing that ridiculous gown like it was something special, her golden curls falling all over her shoulders. She didn't even look like Nora. Nora used to look so pale and sickly and white, and this woman staring at him like he was shit was all healthy and rosy and golden-haired.

He shook his head to clear his brain. "Get up."

"I can't. My balance is off with the ropes."

A small grin crossed Dale's face, revealing his broken teeth. With a brutal yank, he pulled her to her feet and then slapped her across the face. The blow made her fall down again.

He repeated the lifting and slapping again. "Say you're sorry."

Again, he repeated the lifting and hitting. "Say you are afraid."

She was silent, and this time the blow was even harder, making her head snap back.

He lifted her up and hissed right in her face. "Say I'm your master!"

Nora's eyes flew open, and she felt pure rage. She had one master and it wasn't this idiot. With careful aim, she head butted his chin and he screamed in pain, accidently letting her go. She fell and forced herself to scramble away, trying to escape. She didn't get far.

Dale was standing over her, with the shotgun pumped and ready. "Say I'm your master. Say it!" he bellowed like an angry bull.

Nora smiled up at him. "I have one master, and it isn't you."

"Thank you, Nora." There was real joy in Eros' voice. "I've waited a long time to hear you say that."

Nora felt her heart leap in her breast. Eros had suddenly appeared out of nowhere.

Dale whirled around and screamed in terror. The creature behind him was nine feet tall and had two blue and one red eye. It was one of the aliens he had seen on the night of the accident. There was a smile on his face that scared the hell out of Dale.

Next to the nine foot tall alien, was a man of normal height but oddly white-haired.

"I just checked the man by the truck. He has a concussion, but he will live. But Nora's father is dead. Should we leave him that way?"

Nora thought they would ask her opinion, but Eros was emphatic. "Leave him as he is. The next world is his problem."

Obe pointed to Dale. "And this one."

"Where are you sending Jimmy Brady?"

"To that institution out of this solar system. Their reformation program lasts several hundred Earth years."

Dale was shaking like a leaf. "Don't kill me! Please! I know I'm a bastard!" He fell on his knees and Obe pressed some buttons on his receiver.

Dale began to spin around, slowly at first, and then faster and faster, until he was just a ball of light.

"Say good-bye to Dale." Eros laughed. "No muss, no fuss, as you humans say." He smiled at Nora and helped her off the ground. "I will see you tomorrow. Obe will take over now. It is crucial I return to the mother ship immediately." And then he was gone.

"How did he do that?" she asked Obe.

"He invoked the cloak of invisibility to return quickly. They will beam him up." Obe pulled out a blanket and wrapped it around Nora. Then he tapped his watch and spoke into it. "We must leave this place. Observer 1020, please come to my location."

"Observer 1020?" Nora asked.

"She's a trainee. We have her set up in a flower shop as her cover." He turned toward Nora. "Would you like to say anything to your father?"

Nora thought for a moment. "Yes, please."

She walked over to her mother's grave and carefully removed all the beer bottles and set them aside. When she reached for the damaged geraniums, Obe touched her shoulder.

"Leave it. Observer 1020 will take care of it all."

"Thank you." She knelt down and folded her hands.

"Dear God, please give my father the peace in the next world that he never found here on Earth. And please forgive him his sins. He hurt himself more than he hurt anyone else."

She stood up. Obe took her arm and they walked away.

"I can see that you are at peace, too. Very good."

To her surprise, Harry McKow was sitting up, leaning against the truck. He had a dazed expression on his face. "Did I kill him?" he croaked out.

"No," Obe answered. "Dale Gower hit you and shot Elmer Dawson with your gun. Then he ran away. I don't think anyone will ever see Dale again. We have a witness. She called an ambulance. It will be here soon."

Harry reached out and grabbed Nora's hand. "I wouldn't have killed you, miss. I swear. I never thought he was that bad a man."

"I know." Nora patted Harry's head.

"And, miss, one more question."

"Yes."

"Is it the concussion, or did I really see… a nine foot, hairless man with three eyes?"

Nora smiled and looked at Obe. He could answer this one.

Chapter 16

It was a narrow road leading out of the cemetery. One van and one black pickup truck were pulled over. The first one was labeled *Sunflower Florist.*

"Good. Meliandra is here, right on time."

Obe escorted Nora to the pickup and opened the passenger door. At the same time, a teenager jumped out of the driver's side.

"Hi, Obe," the boy said. "Keys are in the ignition."

He didn't seem to be surprised to see Nora, barefoot and dirty, in a hospital gown.

"Thanks, Jason," Obe said. "I have to see Meliandra a moment."

"No rush," Nora said quietly. She was still shaken up by the shooting. She watched as Jason jumped into the flower van, and Obe went to the driver's side to talk to the woman he called Meliandra. Nora guessed it had to be Observer 1020.

Obe was back in a moment. He swung into the driver's seat, started the pickup, and continued out of the cemetery.

"I take it Meliandra is Observer 1020."

"Yes. Her shop is on the Berlin Road."

Nora's head wrinkled in thought. "That's a pretty deserted road. All farmland with occasional woods. She can't get much business."

Obe laughed. "That's the plan. The less business, the better."

"What about the boy named Jason? He looks pretty human to me."

Obe nodded In agreement as he turned the pickup onto the main road of Ridge Valley. "He is. He's a good kid but not very aware. Meliandra pays him well to help her and he doesn't ask any questions."

"So there are a lot of humans who know about Eluvians and other space folk," Nora mused.

"Not a lot, but we have selected a few, here and there. Ridge Valley is a hot spot for us—a lawyer and his wife, Jason, and now you four women." Obe glanced at her. "By the way, Meliandra is not an Eluvian. She comes from the planet Meli that rotates around the star Lotta, in the galaxy Buttana. The Meli are allies with the Eluvians. We work together on many projects. Meli is almost identical to Earth, and so they are eager to study the problems Earth is facing, such as global warming."

"I think I have much to learn," Nora muttered, shaking her head.

A moment later, he updated her on her own situation. "All is set with the hospital and what has happened at the cemetery. There was a bit of an argument, but the authorities soon saw it our way. Since you were kidnapped on their premises, you could sue the hospital. By the time our lawyer was done with both the hospital, the cops, and the press, everyone was glad to just let you go. Gilly and Rose will go home tomorrow," he explained on the ride home.

"I have a lawyer?"

"Yes. I just told you. He was picked up by other Eluvians

when he was in college. A drug trip gone seriously wrong. We saved him and his girlfriend, and now they are on our payroll. I'll deal with him."

"I'll have to clean up a big mess when I get home," Nora thought out loud as they turned onto her street.

"No need. The lawyer's wife owns a cleaning company. She's been inside, got groceries, and been feeding Muffin."

Nora's face broke into a wide grin. "Muffin!"

Obe let her off at the door, and she raced to the door. "Watch the news. Tonight. 7:00 p.m. on channel 10.

"Okay!" Nora waved to him and then unlocked the. door.

"Muffin!" she cried out in joy and the little dog flew into her arms.

Chapter 17

After a warm welcome from Muffin, Nora took a look around. Her house was spotless, not a trace of Dale Gower to be found. Flowers, in careful arrangements, were in her bedroom and living room. A quick check told her that her plants had been watered. Meliandra, she guessed. The fridge was full, and there was wine cooling in the fridge. Also, there was a note on the kitchen table. It was in an odd penmanship, but what could she expect from an Eluvian?

Dear Nora,
I hope all is to your satisfaction. Food, wine, Muffin.
There is champagne also chilling in the refrigerator for tomorrow.
Eros will be arriving in mid-afternoon.
Your good friend.
Obe

It was wonderful to be home.

It was even more wonderful to be home without the fear

of Dale Gower suddenly appearing at her door. She realized that she had been living in fear for a long time and suppressing her feelings. But those days were gone.

After a long, soaking bath, she poured a glass of white wine and settled in front of the television. Obe had been clear in his instructions: 7:00 p.m. Channel 10. She picked up Muffin and relaxed.

The news came on, and Nora was shocked to find out she was part of the lead story. The female anchor faced the camera with excitement.

"Good evening. As we begin, we have two breaking news stories."

The camera panned to the hospital where Gilly and Rose were resting and where Nora had landed.

"For the last week, we have been following a missing persons story. Four women, allegedly abducted by aliens, disappeared after a car accident. Well, tonight, we can report that all four have returned. Jessie Lawrence was found on the side of the road by a trucker and taken to Ridge Valley Hospital. She is in good condition and expected to be released tomorrow. Gilly Roberts, Rose Rillol, and Nora Dawson Glower all reappeared at St. Luke's hospital about seventy miles away. The women had clearly been in a car accident, and doctors think they are all suffering from differing levels of amnesia, but all are expected to recover."

There was a break for a commercial and the anchor was back.

"Our other breaking news story is the murder of a vagrant in Ridge Valley Cemetery this afternoon. Elmer Dawson, a former resident of Ridge Valley, was shot dead while mourning at his wife's grave. A reliable witness said that she witnessed the killing. We have her telling her story."

It was obviously Meliandra. A tall, thin, shockingly white woman with wispy brown hair, dressed in jeans and a t-shirt, came on the screen.

The reporter began, "Why were you here at the cemetery?"

Meliandra pushed back a strand of hair. *"I own Sunflower Florist and I have clients who hire me to spiff up the graves. When I arrived today, I saw a young man, twenty something, fire a gun at the man by the grave. Then he ran into the woods on the east side of the cemetery and disappeared. I called 911 and then saw another man lying injured by his truck."*

The reporter turned to the camera. *"The injured man is Harry McKow, who owns McKow Feed Store. According to his son, he is expected to make a full recovery. But in an odd twist of fate, this story links back to the first one we covered tonight. The murdered man is Elmer Dawson, the father of Nora Dawson, who was one of the missing women. And the killer, identified here by Meliandra, was Nora's ex-husband, Dale Glower.*

The anchor looked shocked. *"Was Nora Dawson involved?"*

"Not at all. She was in St. Luke's Hospital." The reporter shrugged. *"Just an odd twist of fate."*

The anchor laughed. *"Well, I guess so. Those two stories are out of this world."*

Nora switched channels and then hugged Muffin. "Boy, Muffin, that anchor was more right than she could possibly know,."

Eros would come to her.

She slept like a baby, with Muffin curled at her feet.

Chapter 18

The next day dawned sunny and bright. Nora prepared for Eros carefully. A hot bath and a scented hair wash, creams and a light perfume, a manicure and pedicure kept her busy in preparation for her lover's arrival. Satisfied, she brushed her hair and slipped into a silk robe the color of the summer sky.

She would wait for Eros in her small garden under an apple tree. The chair had an extra comfy pillow. Relaxed and happy, she drifted off to sleep.

Eros found her there, under the tree, and ran his fingers through her golden curls. He was invisible.

Nora woke up immediately and opened her eyes. "Where are you?" She knew immediately it was Eros.

"Right here." He took her hand. "Let's go inside."

"Why are you invisible?"

"I cloaked myself so I wouldn't scare your neighbors. In case you haven't noticed, the woman across the street has been watching you with binoculars. You are big news, you know."

"Snoopy woman." Nora laughed. "You should have

appeared and scared the hell out of her." She led him into the bedroom and he immediately materialized.

She threw back her head and drank in the sight of him. He was clad in a loosely tied white robe. It did nothing to hide his magnificence! Nine feet tall, a body of pure muscle and unbridled sexuality, his blue eyes flashed sparks of desire as he raked his gaze over her lush body. The red eye was strangely still.

"Today, we make love, and it is just for us," he whispered hoarsely.

"I know. I can't wait. I'm totally ready." Nora pushed the palms of her hands against his warm chest. "Take me now."

His next words brought her to her knees. "We can't."

"What!" Looking up at him, Nora was shocked beyond belief. "I don't understand."

He scooped her up and sat on the bed, placing her on his knee. "First, we must talk." His hand slipped between the folds of her robe and began to massage her breasts.

"Don't tease me, Eros!" Nora pleaded. "I am so ready for you."

"Are you really?" he teased. "Let me see."

Nora pushed him farther away and made to get off the bed, but one powerful arm reached out and pulled her onto her back. She was helpless in his grasp.

Eros straddled her and actually laughed in her face. "I'm your master. You have said so." He kissed her again, and her heart began to thud a little more quickly. "Do you understand me, Nora?" His lips moved to her neck and nibbled lightly on her delicate skin. "Answer me?"

She tried to bolt, resisting the wonderful feeling of his lips on her skin.

His response was instantaneous. In one movement, he raised his hips enough to flip her hard on her stomach and then peeled her robe from her body. Still straddling her, he gave her naked buttocks a firm smack.

Nora yelped. "Stop that."

"Let us see just how ready you are for me?" he teased.

When she said nothing, he gave her another firm slap that made her buttocks sting. She felt so humiliated, but in a crazy way, she was getting aroused by his power over her. He was so strong and so warm.

"You make me feel so powerless," she whispered out in a strangled voice.

"Of course, I am powerful and strong. But you should feel safe because of that. I would fight your whole world for you."

His words lit a flame deep within her and she sighed. It wasn't lost on Eros. He gave her one more slap, more play than discipline, and slipped his hand between her legs. "You are getting wet, darling. Hot and wet. And I can smell your body preparing to fuck me." His voice was low and hot as he leaned over her and whispered into her ear, "You desire me, Nora."

"No! Not now!" she protested, but she knew it was a lie. His slaps, dominating her, had lit waves of excitement in her body. When he eased down and began to kiss her buttocks with a tenderness she hadn't expected, she knew she was getting too wet to hide.

He read her mind. He inserted one finger in her pussy and gently rubbed her. She felt so helpless, yet so desirable, and hot… hot for Eros.

"The vials have done their work. You are soft and pliant. You will be able to take me into your cunt. I am big, but I think you will manage."

When he gently lifted her onto her back, she looked up with him with hooded eyes, her breathing ragged. "Now?"

"No. We must talk."

She groaned with frustration. "What must we talk about?"

He dragged her back onto his knee and she realized, from his expression, that this talk was serious.

"Okay, I'm all ears."

Eros looked at her blankly "No, you are not."

"It's a phrase. Just go on."

Eros was serious. More serious than Nora had ever seen him.

Her heart was pounding. Something momentous had happened. She could sense it. Eros pulled her close and she reveled in his manly, clean, powerful scent. "What is it? You can tell me anything."

"Eros Commander X had all captains return to the mother ship for a special council meeting. It was long and arduous because we had to transfer data to Eluvia. I won't bore you with all the details."

Nora's eyes widened with hope. "What is it, Eros? What decision? Can I come with you? Has Eros Commander X changed his mind?"

"No, my princess. Not now. Probably not in your lifetime."

Nora's hope drained out of her, replaced with concern. She knew he was leaving her, and she could accept it, although it broke her heart. But now something else had happened. Something serious had occurred at the meeting aboard the mother ship. She remembered how rattled Tria had been. When Tria's little ball feet didn't touch the ground, something was up.

"This is very important, Nora."

"I'm listening."

"The final decision had been made to begin mating with humans on a very small scale. The Voice, as Jessie calls her Eluvian, has agreed. And so have I. But only if you are willing." His hands grasped the mass of golden curls on her head and forced her to meet his gaze.

Nora couldn't speak. She was so shocked by his words and so joyous.

"I'm serious. Do you want to have sex, which we can do, and it will be wonderful, or do you want to mate with me and have my children?" His eyes probed into hers. "It is a little different with Eluvian mating. We would have intercourse, but at the end, it would become more intense. It is not for the faint of heart."

"You are asking me to mate with you to produce Earth/Eluvian children?"

"Yes. But only if you are willing." He shook his mammoth head. "No! Not only willing. But fiercely eager. This will affect your whole life and I will only be here to see you once a year. All your material needs will be met, and an Observer will be assigned to take care of all things. I believe it will be Obe. He has already signed on. Eluvians disguised as humans will attend the birth and make all the alignments that will make the child or children look normal to outsiders."

She stared at him, astounded. A family with Eros was more than she had ever allowed herself to dream about.

"Yes! Oh, yes!"

He took her in his arms and held her close. "Oh, my darling, then we begin."

"Yes. We begin," she echoed, reaching out to hold him tight.

Chapter 19

Eros was everything a male should be if the male was a force of nature created to control everything around him—masculine, powerful, and totally focused on her. "You are ready, my darling?" he asked one more time.

"Yes, I am."

With that, he encircled her waist and began to cradle her, touching her breasts, then her pussy. He began to stroke her with his fingers, making her wet and wild. Then he pulled her thighs apart. "Relax, my darling. I won't hurt you. I promise." From head to foot, he pulsated with a glowing energy that had her in thrall. His muscles were superhuman, bulging and powerful. They rippled with controlled energy.

Nora groaned with growing desire. Her eyes half open, lids heavy, she ran her tongue across her lips. "I want to shatter around you. I want to hold you close as you come inside me. I want you to make me lose myself in your body. I want you to scream with desire like I feel now." She gazed up at him, bulging muscles, hot skin, and a cock thicker and longer than she could ever have imagined. Instinctively, her legs parted under him. "You will kill me. You are too big," she whispered, even hotter with desire than before.

"You will take me, all of me, and cry out with joy," Eros assured her. He began to circle her clit with his index finger, holding her lips apart.

She squirmed and whimpered because it was so intimate and powerful. Her hips arched upward and down, and he circled a little faster, before gently pulling on the strands of her pubic hair.

"Farther apart now," he commanded, pulling her thighs apart. "We need room to play, don't we, little one?"

She obeyed, trembling almost uncontrollably.

"Are you afraid?"

"Yes, a little. So big!" she whispered hoarsely, taking his throbbing cock in her small hands.

He moaned with desire and repositioned himself. The tip of his cock entered her vagina and she felt him begin to push, slowly, but resolutely.

"Don't be scared," he whispered into her ear. "The lotion in the vials have softened and expanded you. I feel your cunt opening up to me. Slowly, but completely."

She felt the same sensations, too, and gasped with pleasure. He was so hard and so big, but her body was contouring around him, pulling him inside her even as he pushed forward. "Oh, my goodness! Nothing like this has ever happened to me before," she gasped. She arched her back, eyes wide, and gasped for breath.

His own blue eyes were startlingly clear and strong. The light within him seemed to intensify, his gaze on her body now a glow of desire that burned her skin. The red eye blinked rapidly. Eros' smile was crooked. "Earth woman, my desire for you has lit me from within. Can you feel the fire of desire you have kindled within me?

She didn't, couldn't, answer. Gasping for breath, she could only hang on for dear life.

He pushed harder and she gave out a little scream of pleasure. When he began to rock back and forth, the motion deep within her found a spot that she never knew existed and tingling waves of heat began to pulse through her pussy. Her excitement increased as she heard Eros groan and groan again with his own wild sensations.

"I'm all in," he hissed with excitement.

"I feel like I will explode with pleasure, alien man!" Nora cried out.

"Not completely, human woman!" he cried out. He began to rock faster and faster as his hand rubbed her clit until she was bouncing off the bed in a mindless dance of sexual union.

"Stop! Stop!" she begged, praying he would not listen to her pleas.

"Never. Never!" He grasped her hips and braced her body so she couldn't escape. Her own little hands cupped his buttocks, squeezing and holding on for dear life.

"I want to come!" she screamed. "My body is burning. I'll go crazy if I don't come!"

"I'm going to make you come, but it will be my way. I will make you come like we do in my world. Every cell in your body will feel like the cells of your clit."

Nora's eyes flew open to see the blue of his eyes turn to burning coals. He was hot and wild, and she knew she was completely in his power. He had lost control, and so she would see!

"You want it, don't you?" he cried out.

The pleasure turned to fire in her body, and she pushed down, matching him thrust for thrust.

Eros groaned. "That's it, that's it. I feel a spot deep within you, pulsing, eager for release!"

She couldn't answer. She was burning with the heat of their joint passion. It was heaven!

"More! Faster! Faster!" she moaned, and he upped the pace of his thrusting.

"Grasp the hilt of my cock. Grasp it!" he growled. "I want to flood you with cum and make my babies in your beautiful body, so smooth and delicate and wild with desire."

Something wild was happening to them. Heads thrown back and gasping for air, they began to break the chains of gravity, and as one entity, they rose up, spinning in a circle.

Eros laughed with sheer joy and the sound of his pleasure inflamed her as he thrust into her again. And again. And again.

It was all she needed. The spot he had found deep within her exploded like fireworks in the night sky. Her head rose and fell against his chest as the indescribably wonderful waves of orgasm ripped through her body.

She vibrated with pleasure as she came again and again, buckling up to his body, her vagina tightening and then releasing, tightening and releasing. Her reflexes were primal, beyond her control. It was unending and each spasm was greater than the one before.

He bit into her neck, his lips searing hot as his teeth broke the skin. And then they were one, Nora and Eros, lovers aflame. Male and female, human and alien, woman and master, all disappeared to become one fiery light forged in passion. It was so intense, it lifted them off the ground and they began to spin, slowly, then faster and wild through the lights of the universe.

Faster and faster! Spinning together.

"Nora," he rasped into her ear. "Are you ready? No going back now!"

"Yes! Yes! Yes!"

"It will be hot, hotter than you've ever felt! We don't know how many children we will create."

"I don't care! Don't stop," she begged.

"We are going to spin faster and faster, and with each turn, more of you will become your clit."

"How..." But her breath was gone and she couldn't finish the sentence.

His voice was harsh with desire. "This is how we impregnate and create life in my world. Faster and faster, we will spin, finally exploding into the white light of creation. We will be joined together, a racing comet speeding across the night sky in a ball of flame."

Nora couldn't answer. Her head flew back and she felt herself flying like a comet in the star-filled sky. Her whole body was getting hotter and hotter. His cock was moving, propelling them around and around and he was screaming with the sheer joy of it. She screamed, too, as they became one living being. Until they finally reached the point when they disappeared into each other.

It was a climax so blindingly bright that Nora knew what it was to actually explode with passion. Eros pulled his hands through her hair, their legs plastered together and entwined, as they spun faster and faster through the air, her orgasm never ending... and his culminating in a roar of passion that vibrated the entire room as he reached the uppermost pinnacle of desire and shuddered his way into the ultimate pleasure.

Totally sated and still throbbing with the intensity of their lovemaking, Nora and Eros lay on the bed. She was cradled in his powerful arms. Never in her life had she felt so safe. So right.

"I love you, "she whispered.

He was silent for a long time. He pulled her hands to his chest and his blue eyes were brilliant blue. But to her shock, the red eye was closed. "I have come to love you, Nora. Your gentleness and kindness make me wistful for your respect, even as you have come to respect my power and courage."

Nora let her head rest on his chest. "Always. You have my respect, and you have my love."

"I know. And I love you, too."

She nuzzled his throat with her lips. "I love you, my master. My master and my hero."

Then a thought occurred to her and she giggled.

Eros gave her a little hug. "What is so funny?"

"I wonder how many children we will have?"

Chapter 20

F ive.
    The answer to the question she asked Eros was five.

Five children, all girls.

Each one looked just like her, born with a golden curl on the top of her head. All of them were born with Eros' flashing blue eyes, tamed down a bit so as not to scare any curious onlookers.

So far there weren't too many. Ordinarily, quintuplets would be a big story, but Obe made sure that other events occupied the press each time they got too close. Their external third eyes had been removed before birth by gene editing. To the whole world, they looked entirely human, although once in a while Nora could see Eros in them. Once an Eluvian gynecologist, disguised as a human, had delivered them, an Eluvian pediatrician then took over their care. Nora was surprised to discover just how many Eluvians disguised as humans were on Earth. They kept to themselves but still blended into the local community.

Now in their nursery, Nora smiled and gave each one of

them a kiss. They were her darlings, and she was the brood mother she had always wanted to be. When Eros came for his next visit, he would be so proud.

They had moved, of course. Ridge Valley was still in the headlights of every UFO hunter, government agency, and press stringer in the nation.

Nora only insisted on one thing before they left Ridge Valley. She hired a stonemason to make two head stones, one for her mother and one for her father.

The funeral had been private. It was just Obe, Nora, Gilly, Rose, and Jessie. Meliandra supplied the flowers and the long term contract to keep the graves maintained and spiffy.

Heavily pregnant, Nora had cried for both her parents, but her new knowledge of how the universe worked tempered her loss. As Tria had told her, 'Energy never dies, it just changes form.' When a beam of light crossed her face at her mother's grave, Nora knew that she was out there somewhere.

Berga Stiven Dawson
   Beloved Mother
   Born September 2, 1976 Stockholm, Sweden
   Died November 1, 2013
   Always In My Heart – Nora

Farther down, in another row, Nora had them bury her father.

Elmer Dawson
   1971-2021
   He Lived As He Died

. . .

Thelma had been invited.

She declined to attend, or to give back the fund money raised for Nora. No one was surprised.

Obe had found all four women, Jessie, Nora, Gilly, and Rose, a place where people tended to keep to themselves and not ask a lot of questions. Small town New Englanders, as a rule, didn't bother anyone else who paid taxes, kept to the law, and didn't cause a bother. Gilly, Rose, Jessie, and Nora were all new residents who fit those rules, and everyone was happy. So, if they seemed a little odd, people were too polite to ask any questions.

Obe had provided them all with new identities. They were blending in, and it helped that their new hometown was a beacon for many alien residents. Meliandara's sister, Felicity, ran her own flower business down the road. Like her sister's establishment, it was off the beaten track and didn't advertise for business.

"We Eluvians are very adaptable," Obe had explained. "There are several tech billionaires who are Eluvians, as well as two members of Congress. And don't get me started about the music world."

But now it was almost eight o'clock and she would be late for Jessie's party. Nora hurried down the stairs of her new home and glanced at the mirror in the hall of the center.

"Who's this doll in the mirror?" she asked herself with a laugh. "Not the old Nora for sure." The old Nora, white-blonde hair, white skin, a tad heavy and dressed in boring neutrals that kept her from standing out in a crowd was long gone.

The new Nora's reflection was happy, curious, and confident. Her skin was rosy with good health, and her blonde hair flowed to her shoulders in a mass of golden curls that fell to the top of her red cashmere sweater. The sweater accented her full breasts and small waist. With it, she had chosen a black skirt, black tights, and black high heels. Gold bangles the color of her hair shone at her ears, neck and wrists.

She was a knockout!

Eros had told her his work would transform her and he hadn't been kidding. Classes in karate, judo, and yoga had given her body good tone. She looked athletic and powerful. Especially since she gave birth only six weeks ago.

She and Jessie and Gilly were all mothers. Rose had opted out of a domestic life but seemed to very happy in work.

Speaking of friends, she had better get going. Jessie was having a housewarming in her new home, and Nora didn't want to be late. She had debated bringing the babies but decided against it. The fall night was chilly, and the children, who looked totally human, were really half-human and half-Eluvian, and needed a lot more sleep than the average baby.

"Tria. I have to get going!" she called out. "I already said goodnight to the girls."

Tria appeared at the top of the stairs. She wore a woolen cap over her head, to hide her antennae, and a long dress that hid the narrowness of her purple/black body. Her ball feet were stuck in high top sneakers. When she went out in the daytime, she wore sunglasses to hide her yellow eyes, and a scarf covered her third eye. There was no doubt she was unusual. But being New Englanders, everyone was too polite to comment.

Only one human had had the nerve to approach her. One woman came right up and confronted her. "Madam, you are seriously anorexic."

Tria had taken off her sunglasses and stared at the woman with her yellow eyes and the woman has scurried away.

Nora had laughed her head off when Tria indignantly told her the story,

Tria was still grumbling. "We should have moved to New York City. No one comments on anyone there."

"You'd better stay inside." Nora chuckled. "You have enough to do taking care of the children."

Tria was the new nanny for Nora's children. She had eagerly accepted Eros' offer and helped foster their Eluvian side while Nora nurtured the human side of their personalities and bodies.

Tria was a wonderful nanny to the children, and they adored her. Now she whistled and a large mound of white fur scuttled down the stairs. Borgo.

One foot high, with six legs and four ears, it was vital to keep him under wraps. Luckily, for security and sharp-eyed neighbors, Borgos didn't like to go outside. Tria usually walked Borgo and Muffin at night when no one was around.

"I won't be long," Nora assured her.

"Don't worry. I won't be joining the bats until after midnight," Tria said crisply.

"How is the study progressing?" Nora asked, slipping into her black coat. She knew that besides being a nanny to the girls, Tria was working on a study of bats for the Eluvian Scientific Data Program, also known as ESDP.

"Very well. Over half of them have agreed to give DNA samples. I'm setting it up with the mother ship. Taking the samples will be a big undertaking."

Nora was just going to agree when Muffin came flying into the hall, dragging his leash along.

"There you are, you little devil." Nora laughed. She attached the leash to his collar. "I'll take him with me tonight."

"Very good."

Nora slipped the end of the leash around her wrist, grabbed her car keys, and went out onto the porch. It was a beautiful night, clear and crisp. The sweet smell of apples from their tree permeated the night. She inhaled the wonderful scent while Muffin waited patiently by her side.

"The Earth is a wonderful place, isn't it, Tria?" Nora said. It wasn't really a question.

Tria had followed Nora out onto the porch. She looked up at the night sky.

"It certainly is. I'm glad I decided to come with you and take care of Eros' children."

"My children, too," Nora reminded her with a laugh.

"Of course," Tria agreed. "But to me, they will always be little Eluvians."

Nora nodded. She could understand Tria's point of view.

"Where is Observer Obe?" Tria asked. "This is a great night for transmission beams from Eluvia."

"I'm meeting him at Jessie's party. He's bringing Felicity and the wine. Such a good human, isn't he? Did you hear that the FBI offered him a job? They thought he would make such a good undercover agent."

Tria made a scathing sound. "Such a good actor, you mean. If they only knew. He is bound for great universal success, but he will stay here with you and the girls for now. He really loves you and Jessie and Gilly and Rose. Eros made a good decision when he chose Obe to watch over you all."

"Yes, he did. Eros deserves to be the master of his ship and the master of my heart."

Tria smiled. "Will Obe be returning with you tonight?"

Nora sighed with disappointment. "No. Rose put in first dibs for him so—"

'I can always summon someone. There is a group of Lodi from the Constellation Pirus."

Nora hesitated. She loved sex now, but sometimes Tria was a bit too adventurous. The last match resembled a pogo stick too much.

"I'll pass. Tonight."

She had another reason. Eros had spoiled her for other lovers. Sometimes she let Obe please her, but it was really Eros she was thinking about. She loved Eros, and she was content in the love he could offer to her. What more could she ask for than his love?

She giggled and looked up. Tria was right. It was a clear night outside, full of stars and an almost full harvest moon. They both studied the panoply of the universe above them. So many planets, so many stars, so many galaxies. The universe was mind boggling.

Tria was unusually sentimental. "All my siblings are up there, not to mention six-hundred of my children."

Nora was stunned. "You never told me you had children. And six hundred!"

Tria laughed. "Yes. It's a little different up there, and I was a lot younger. Your five are enough for me right now, although the bat king in a Central American cave system has made me an interesting offer. I might take a vacation when Eros returns and go visit him."

Nora smiled. "That's good, Tria. I'm glad you are making friends here on Earth." She looked up at the sky and waved.

"He'll be home soon," Tria said softly. "You'll be back in Eros' arms before you know it."

Tria went back in the house, and Nora walked across the gravel path to her car, where she paused for a moment and, again, raised her face to the moonlit sky. Her lips lifted into a smile. Eros was somewhere in the vastness of space, working his way back to her.

"I can't wait. My darling lord and master." She blew Eros a kiss. "Come home soon."

Lys Britdotter

Lys Britdotter loves astronomy, oceanography, history, and travel -any place, anywhere, any time! Wings clipped by Covid, she has turned to the wild world of sci-fi romance, where anything is possible. An experienced writer of romance, historical romance, and non-fiction work, she is very proud of Call Me Jezebel, the first book in a four- part series on alien visitation and romance on planet earth.

Animal rescue, her darling children, and very loving husband are the only distractions she is now allowing to keep her from her computer. When she has writer's block, she makes homemade soups, and paints; cats are her favorite subjects. She used her portrait of Aldo, her white rescue, as her bio photo.

Don't miss these exciting titles by Lys Britdotter and Blushing Books!

Star Lovers Series
Call Me Jezebel
Naughty Nora

Blushing Books

Blushing Books is the oldest eBook publisher on the web. We've been running websites that publish steamy romance and erotica since 1999, and we have been selling eBooks since 2003. We have free and promotional offerings that change weekly, so please do visit us at http://www.blushingbooks.com/free.

Blushing Books Newsletter

Please join the Blushing Books newsletter
to receive updates & special promotional offers.
You can also join by using your mobile phone:
Just text **BLUSHING** to 22828.

Every month, one new sign up via text messaging will receive
a $25.00 Amazon gift card, so sign up today!